Tower of Darkness

Gulf Coast Paranormal
Season Three Book One

By M. L. Bullock and Kevin D. Bullock

Prologue—Helene—1723

As the sun began its descent behind the sprawling oaks and Spanish moss, the air in Mobile turned cool and heavy with the scent of the river. I made my way along the cobbled streets, the hem of my dress whispering against the stones, an uneasy feeling settling in the pit of my stomach.

It was not just the chill of the evening that caused me to shiver, but the shift in the air, a tension that seemed to tighten around me with each step.

The townsfolk, with whom I had shared many a pleasant nod or exchange in greetings, now turned their gazes away as I passed by them. Where there had once been smiles and warm welcomes, there were now only shadows and silence.

The whispers began to weave around me, a tapestry of suspicion and fear, their words obscured but their meaning clear. "...that woman, the Protestant..." I heard someone mutter from a darkened doorway, their voice laced with a mix of curiosity and disdain.

Approaching my home, the familiar sight of Mrs. Leclerc, the baker, should have offered some comfort. Yet, as our eyes met, there was a flicker of something unspoken, a barrier erected where none had been before.

"Good evening, Mrs. Leclerc," I ventured, my voice steady despite the turmoil within. I smiled in a friendly manner but my effort was met with silence.

She only responded with a hushed prayer, her eyes darting away to the cobblestones beneath our feet. No greeting returned, no acknowledgment of the bond we had once shared. It was as if the very air around us had grown thick with unvoiced accusations, and I stood accused by silence alone.

I continued on, the sense of unease growing with each passing moment. The whispers seemed to follow, carried on the wind, as if the town itself had taken up a silent chant against me. It was in this twilight, between the light of day and the shadows of evening, that the fabric of my world began to unravel.

As I reached the door to the home I shared with Francis, I paused, a deep sense of foreboding washing over me.

The warmth that usually greeted me felt distant now, as if a chill had settled over everything I held dear.

I could not yet see the storm that was brewing on the horizon, but I could feel it in the whispers of the wind, in the averted gazes of my neighbors, in the silence that weighed heavier than any spoken threat.

It was in this moment, standing on the threshold of my own home, that I realized how fragile the peace I had known truly was. The world I had entered, bound by love and shared dreams with Francis, was now a place of unseen dangers, where fear festered in whispered words and suspicion lurked in every shadow. I had made a horrible mistake by leaving France. My mother pleaded with me to stay but I had followed my heart, fool that I am.

As I stepped inside, the warmth of the hearth did little to dispel the cold that had taken root in my heart. Francis was yet to return, and the house felt all the emptier for it.

I lit a candle, its flickering light casting shadows that danced across the walls, as if echoing the unrest that danced through my thoughts. Where were the servants? Why were the lamps out?

In the quiet of our home, I could no longer deny the storm that was coming.

The whispers, the looks, the sudden coldness—it all pointed to a tempest on the verge of breaking. And I, at its heart, could only wait and wonder how the love I bore my husband, how my faith, could have led me here, to the edge of a precipice from which there seemed no turning back.

France may as well have been a million miles away.

As the candlelight flickered, casting long shadows across the room, the front door screeched open, startling me from my reverie. It was Francis, his face etched with worry and urgency.

"Helene," he breathed, his voice a blend of relief and fear as he stepped inside, locking the door behind him. The warmth of his presence did little to quell the growing storm within me. "Helene, my love," he began again, taking my hands in his, his eyes searching mine for understanding. "The town... they're calling for blood. Your faith, our union—it has roused a fear I cannot quell."

His words tumbled out, each one a blow to the hope I've clung to. "Why would you bring me to this place? How could you let this happen?" I felt desperate but more than that, Francis, my beloved was not strong enough to protect me from the crowds.

"If you would reconsider, Helene. Reconsider your faith. That's all it would take. That would appease the priest and the rest of the townspeople. Please, Helene. For your sake, for mine."

"I pray for you, Francis. You know what I believe—what you used to believe! How you have changed! And now I have your child in my womb! You betray me, husband! You have betrayed me!"

I felt the weight of his gaze, heavy with the burden of decisions made and the consequences now upon us. "You must leave, Helene. Tonight," he urged, his grasp tightening. "I cannot protect you from them. Stay gone until dawn, wife."

The very air seemed to thin, a chill settled between us, as if his words had invited the cold from outside into our home, into our lives. I stared back at him, disbelief and fear mingling with the love I held for this man. How could I still love him? He had abandoned our mutual faith and now was abandoning me. Tears streamed down my face.

"Leave? And go where, Francis? To be alone and hunted?"

He pulled me close, his voice a whisper against my hair. "The swamp. It will hide you until I can make them see reason. Please,

Helene, for us, for our future. For our child. Go to the heart of the swamp and wait for the sun."

With a heart heavy as stone, I made the choice to flee into the night.

Francis led me to the back door, pressing a small, cloth-wrapped bundle into my hands—provisions for my flight. Had he planned this all along? Our goodbye was a silent pact of hope and desperation, sealed with a kiss that spoke of a thousand unspoken promises and fears.

Yes, I loved him still and he loved me. He must love me!

I opened the back door and it creaked open, revealing the dense shadows of the forest beyond our home. I stepped into the darkness, the cool night air wrapping around me like a shroud. Again I wondered where my servants had gone? I didn't think to ask Francis. There was no time.

Behind me, the door closed with a soft thud, a sound final and foreboding.

I moved quickly, guided by the moon's pale light filtering through the trees. The sounds of the night enveloped me—the distant hoot of an owl, the rustle of leaves underfoot, the steady beat of my own heart, were a constant companion.

Francis's warnings echoed in my mind, urging me on when my resolve began to falter.

The swamp loomed ahead, its waters still and silent beneath the moon. I paused at its edge, the reality of my situation settling in. I was alone, a fugitive in a strange land, propelled into the unknown by the very things that defined me—my faith, my love, my very identity.

Drawing a deep breath, I stepped into the swamp, the murky water cold against my skin. Each step was a challenge, the mud clinging to my skirts, pulling me back, as if the land itself wished to keep me rooted in this place of peril and accusation. There was a small island not far from me. If I could get there, I could hide. I lifted the bag of provisions above my head and bit my lip to prevent myself from crying too loudly.

But I pressed on, driven by the need to survive, to return to Francis, to prove our innocence and reclaim the life that was being torn away from us.

The swamp closed around me, a world apart from the one I had known, filled with both danger and the faintest glimmer of hope. I could see the glint of eyes shining in the night. Frogs, snakes and other creatures watched me, an interloper into their realm.

Strangely, I was more afraid of the other humans than any slimy animal I might encounter. I decided the small island was not far enough. I could hear people shouting. Were they calling my name or was I imagining that?

The deeper I ventured into the swamp, the more the natural sounds of the night seemed to give way to an eerie silence. My heart raced, not just from fear of what human pursuers might do, but from the sense of entering a realm that was not entirely of this world.

Suddenly, a soft glow appeared ahead, not the silver of moonlight, but a warmer, amber light that seemed to beckon. Drawing closer, I saw it was a lantern, hanging seemingly in midair. At first, I believed that no hand held it, no figure stood by its light, yet it swayed gently as if caught in a breeze I could not feel. As I tentatively drew closer, I recognized Hartee, my servant girl—native of these strange lands.

"Fear not, mistress," whispered a voice, feminine and rich with her familiar accent. The air around me grew warmer, the oppressive feeling of the swamp lessened. "You are not alone."

I reached out, drawn to the light, but as my fingers brushed against the lantern I felt deep sympathy for my servant. "Thank you, Hartee. Thank you. You should go. Don't go back to the village. Run, run far away. What if they find you too? Go home. Go!" I commanded her with tears in my eyes. I did not for one minute believe they would not come for me. I could not live with myself if I was the cause of Hartee's death.

She nodded and then pointed past the cypress we huddled under. "There. Go to that island. No one will go there. Stay in the trees. The creatures in the water, they will eat you if you sleep on the land." I swallowed upon hearing that and watched her splash her way back to the shore.

Exhausted, I pressed on and finally reached the island she indicated, a haven in the midst of danger. The ground was firmer here, and I allowed myself a moment to rest, to lay down my bundle and catch my breath. The sounds of the swamp resumed around me, a chorus of night creatures that seemed less threatening, more a part of the world I now found myself in.

Remembering her warning, I found a tree that appeared easy enough to climb. With my bundle in my teeth, I climbed up and found a somewhat safe spot. I did not want to blow out the lantern but I knew that I must. If I did not, they would find me.

Oh, Mama! How I regret my decision!

As I sat, I couldn't help but reflect on the events that had led me here, to this moment of solitude. I thought of Francis, of the love we shared in France, and the turmoil that now tore us apart.

The reality of my situation weighed heavily on me, yet I found a strange comfort in the solitude of the swamp. It was as if in this place, far removed from the judgments and fears of the town, I could find a semblance of peace.

I unpacked the small bundle Francis had given me, finding a bit of bread, cheese, and a flask of water. As I ate, I realized this might be the last kindness I would receive for some time. The thought brought tears to my eyes, not just for the love I still felt for Francis, but for the uncertainty of what lay ahead.

What he wanted me to do, renounce my faith, bend the knee to the Catholics, I would never do. To do so, would be to betray the blood of my family, betray my own love for God.

How dare Francis force me to make such a choice?

In the quiet of the night, with the sounds of the swamp as my lullaby, I closed my eyes, the events of the day seemed to recede, and for the first time since the whispers had begun, I felt a measure of peace.

The swamp, with all its mystery and danger, had become my sanctuary, and for now, that was enough.

Chapter One–Midas

There's something to be said about watching your team dangling from ropes, faces set in determination or lit up with laughter. That was my idea behind choosing Rock Out, the climbing gym that's become somewhat of a legend around these parts.

I wanted to shake us out of our usual haunts, literally and figuratively, and it seemed like watching each other grapple with gravity was just the ticket. Of course, not everyone was having it.

From the ground, I watched as Sierra attempted yet another climb. Her determination was palpable, even if her skills didn't quite match up. Petite and blonde, she usually maneuvered through life with a kind of graceful ease on high heels, but rock climbing had her beaten, at least for now. Maybe she should have worn those high heels instead of climbing gear.

Joshua, ever the supportive husband, shadowed her ascent, ready to catch her or cheer her on, whichever was needed first. He shook his head good-naturedly when she failed to reach the next handhold but if he was frustrated, he didn't let it show. Well, not much.

Around us, the gym buzzed with the energy of people pushing their limits, the air filled with the scent of chalk and the sound of hands slapping against holds.

I couldn't help but smile, seeing my team like this—out of the dark, haunted places we usually found ourselves in, and into a space that was bright, loud, and alive. Jericho was a natural athlete, but Macie had to stand on the ground to plot her ascent before she even got started.

There were moments of levity, a brief respite from the night shadows we regularly chased.

In the back of my mind, I knew these moments were precious, fleeting. Our work didn't allow for many of them. Yet, here we were, finding joy amidst the challenge, strength in our struggles. Cassidy squeezed my hand before she kissed my cheek and cheered on the group.

I leaned back against a cool, concrete wall, arms crossed, a small, contented smirk playing on my lips. This was more than just team building; it was a reminder of the lighter side of life, a contrast to the darkness we so often faced.

Little did I know, as I watched Sierra swear about another slip, that the day's shadows weren't quite done with us yet. Cassidy smiled up at the twisted sight.

"I'm going back up. Poor Sierra. She's literally freaking out."

"That's probably a good idea. It's time to go anyway. You know Little Sister must be the best at everything. Except clearly rock climbing."

Cassidy frowned at me playfully before laughing too. I watched my pretty red headed wife gear up to join Joshua and Sierra on the rock wall. I was disappointed that Chris hadn't shown up but I kind of understood why he wouldn't. His name had been cleared but not his conscious.

The lighthearted atmosphere took a sudden shift when my phone broke the chorus of encouragement and grunts of effort. Pulling it from my pocket, I glanced at the caller ID—Cal Gardner, the manager of the RSA Battle House Tower.

The name alone was enough to wipe the smirk from my lips, replacing it with a line of concern. Cal wasn't the type to call without good reason, especially knowing what my team and I do. He and Papa Angelos had been good friends. The older man had taken it hard when my grandfather passed away.

I excused myself from the group, pressing the phone to my ear as I found a quieter corner. "This is Midas," I answered, keeping my tone even despite the growing knot of anticipation in my stomach.

"Midas, it's Cal. I, uh, I hope I'm not interrupting," his voice came through, tinged with an unmistakable edge of panic. I could almost picture him pacing, running a hand through his gray hair in distress. "We've got—I've got a situation here at the tower. It's... well, it's not good. Unexplainable phenomena if you catch my drift. I need you. Need your help."

The RSA Battle House Tower, a modern monolith against Mobile's skyline, was no stranger to rumors of the paranormal. But for Cal to reach out directly, things must have been dire. My gaze drifted back to my team, their laughter now a distant murmur against the gravity of Cal's words.

"I understand. We can be there within a few hours," I found myself responding, the decision firm. There was no hesitation; this was what we did, why we existed. "Just hold tight, Cal. We're on it."

As I ended the call, the weight of responsibility settled firmly on my shoulders. The transition from leisure to the line of duty was abrupt, a reminder of the unpredictable nature of our work. Jericho won the competition, much to Sierra's complaint, but it was a clear win. Nobody could scale that wall as fast as Jericho, not even Macie who came in second.

Sierra's laughter reached me again, a fleeting sound soon drowned out by the gears shifting in my mind, already moving towards the investigation ahead.

I turned back to the group, my expression serious now, the previous ease gone. It was time to rally the team, to shift from the challenge of rock climbing to the mysteries waiting in the shadows of the RSA Battle House Tower.

This was more than a sudden change of plans; it was a leap back into the unknown, into the darkness we navigated all too well.

Gathering the team around, I couldn't help but notice the shift in atmosphere as their attention turned towards me, curiosity quickly morphing into concern at the sight of my solemn expression. The gym's ambient noise seemed to fade into the background, a stark contrast to the seriousness of our circle.

"We've got a new case," I began, my voice steady, commanding the space. "Cal Gardner from the RSA Battle House Tower just called. They're experiencing some... unexplainable phenomena. And they've asked for our help."

A collective murmur rippled through the group. The tower was well-known among us, not just as a city landmark but as a site of numerous ghost stories and unverified reports of paranormal activity. Its modern façade belied the depth of its haunted reputation, something we had yet to explore ourselves.

Sierra's face was the first to break into a determined look, any residual frustration from her climbing attempts replaced by the focused demeanor of a seasoned investigator.

"What kind of phenomena?" she asked, her tone laced with both excitement and an edge of apprehension. "Apparitions? They must have great security cameras. Do we have video evidence?"

"Cal didn't go into details over the phone, but it sounded serious," I replied, locking eyes with each of them in turn. "He wouldn't have reached out if it wasn't. We need to be prepared for anything."

Jericho, still breathing heavily from his last climb, nodded, his usual joviality replaced by a silent acknowledgment of the weight of our new task. Macie, on the other hand, already seemed to be mentally cataloging potential equipment and research needs, her analytical mind ticking over the possibilities.

Cassidy squeezed my hand again, her earlier light-heartedness gone, replaced by the solid support she always offered. "When do y'all leave?" she asked, voice steady. Her inference was clear. Sierra and I were always the pair to take the interview and do the initial walkthrough.

"As soon as possible. Let's head back, grab some lunch, and Sierra and I will go see what's up. Does that sound like a plan?" I asked already stepping out of the role of team leader at a social outing and back into the role of lead investigator on the brink of a potentially dangerous investigation.

The nods and murmurs of assent told me all I needed to know.

This team, my team, was ready. It was possible that we'd begin investigating tonight but we all had family, and children. Well, most of us.

As we dispersed to gather our things, the weight of leadership pressed down on me, not as a burden, but as a reminder of the trust placed in my hands. The laughter and light-hearted competition of moments ago felt like a distant memory as we stepped back into our real work, the work that eventually waited for us in the shadows and whispers of the RSA Battle House Tower.

Our day of climbing had come to an abrupt end, but a different kind of ascent awaited us—one fraught with unknown dangers and the all-too-familiar thrill of the hunt.

The journey from the bright, echoing space of the gym to the silent, expectant halls of the tower felt like stepping through a veil, from one world into another, a world where the past and the present intertwined in unpredictable, often terrifying ways.

Chapter Two—Sierra

The ride over to the RSA Battle House Tower was filled with a mixture of anticipation and the remnants of our earlier banter about the rock-climbing fiasco. Midas glanced over at me, a smirk playing on his lips, clearly amused by my ongoing grudge against our latest team-building exercise.

"You'll get to pick where we go next time, Little Sister," he promised, his tone teasing yet sincere.

I let out a huff, crossing my arms as I sank a little deeper into the passenger seat. "It better be something that involves less... vertical challenges," I retorted, unable to keep the smile from my voice. Despite the jest, a warm feeling spread through me. This man has been more than just a boss; he was family.

We had seen too much, been through too many dark places together not to be. Midas and Cassidy, Joshua and I—I could barely count how many cases we'd worked together.

As we approached the tower, the lighthearted mood gradually faded, replaced by the weight of our upcoming task. I couldn't help but feel the familiar tug of my psychic senses, a subtle vibration in the air that hinted at the unseen energies swirling around the modern monolith. Yes, it was striking, the tower was beautiful.

It was an odd sensation, one I learned to interpret over the years, signaling that today's investigation won't be straightforward. *Yeah, something was definitely up.* I raised an eyebrow at Midas but didn't say a word about what I was feeling. I preferred to push those "feelings" to the side and pursue the facts first. That's how you undertake paranormal investigations. Or you were supposed to.

Midas pulled into a parking spot, and we gathered our thoughts before stepping out into the bright afternoon. The tower loomed above us, its sleek lines and glass façade hid the secrets we were here to uncover. I couldn't shake the feeling that whatever resided within was already aware of our arrival; it was watching us with unseen eyes.

"It's game time," Midas said, his voice grounding me back to the moment. He was right. We'd faced the unknown before, armed with nothing but our wits, our equipment, and each other. Whatever lay ahead, our team would face it together, as we always had.

But as we walked towards the entrance, I couldn't help but feel the edges of my psychic awareness prickling with alertness. It was going to be one of those days, I thought to myself. The kind where the shadows felt a little too deep, and the whispers of the past were a little too loud.

Cal Gardner was waiting for us at the entrance, the lines of worry etched deeply into his face. I knew him well. Older man, sweet spirit, very polite. Like Papa Angelos, he had that old school vibe. He rose when sitting at the table when a lady was leaving. He opened doors and always had the best of manners.

Next to him stood a woman whose presence seemed to carry its own weight of unease.

Sarah Sylvester, as we were quickly introduced, owned the cleaning crew responsible for maintaining the tower's sheen. The brief flicker of fear that passed over her dark features when she shook my hand was enough to tell me that her experiences here were far from ordinary. She was really experiencing something terrible. And she was terrified.

"You're here," Cal said, a mix of relief and apprehension in his voice. "I can't tell you how much we appreciate you coming so quickly. We appreciate it. I appreciate it."

Sarah nodded in agreement, her gaze shifting nervously towards the upper floors. "It's been... difficult," she admitted, her voice barely above a whisper. "Especially on the lower four floors. There's something not right about this place."

Her confirmation sent a shiver down my spine, an instinctual reaction that had nothing to do with the temperature. Midas squeezed my shoulder, a silent gesture of support. We were about to step into a situation that was rapidly unfolding into something neither of us had truly anticipated. You expect old buildings to make noises, but the tower, it was pretty new.

"Why don't you show us around? Show us where things are happening. Can you describe them?" I took out my digital recorder and got permission to record the interviews. The place was immaculate. From the glass windows to the shiny floors, whatever paranormal activity they were facing, it hadn't affected Sarah's job performance.

Cal explained that the tower had thirty-five floors but the lower four were residential apartments, mainly for seniors. Wealthy seniors, actually. Sarah explained that her crew, Magic Maids, were only responsible for the lower four floors. There was an industrial crew that handled the rest of the building.

As we moved through the lobby, Sarah began to recount her story in more detail. "What I saw, what my daughter saw, was on the fourth floor," she started, her voice steady but haunted. "I saw a face outside the window. But we were so high up, it wasn't possible for anyone to be there. At first, I thought it had to be a reflection but there was no one else there. No one was with us. No one at all. Just the ladies that work with me."

"Are you sure? Nobody snuck a boyfriend in? Someone from one of the other floors maybe?" Midas asked, doing his due diligence, trying to debunk the phenomena. "What did he look like?"

Her description sent my senses into overdrive. I'd heard of apparitions appearing in impossible places before, but there was a palpable fear in Sarah's recounting that made this different. It felt personal, targeted almost. "I couldn't tell you much about him, except his face. It was gray, wrinkled and dirty, like he just dug himself out of the dirt. Black clothing, I think. Yeah, he was wearing black but I couldn't see his clothing clearly. Oh, and he had a hat on. A strange looking hat. You know, the tri cornered kind?"

I shivered visibly as she continued her narrative. "Go on, Sarah. You're doing great. Just share whatever you can remember. No matter how odd it may seem to you."

"Believe it. We have heard everything."

The woman looked tired, like she hadn't slept in ages. My heart went out to her as she sighed and continued. Cal gave her a supportive nod.

"My daughter, Gianna, she's seen more than me," Sarah continued, casting a worried look towards the elevators as if expecting something to emerge at any moment. "She's terrified to come here now. Won't even step foot in the building. My employees don't want to do their job and that's not like them."

Midas exchanged a glance with me, his eyes reflecting my own concern. This wasn't just a simple case of a haunted location; families were being affected; lives disrupted by whatever was lurking within these walls.

We went from floor to floor and the higher we went, the worse I felt.

As we prepared to ascend to the fourth floor, my heart hammered against my ribcage, not just in fear but with a resolve to help. These people were counting on us, on our ability to confront whatever lay ahead.

And as we stepped into the elevator, I could only hope that our preparation would be enough to face the truths hidden in the shadows of the RSA Battle House Tower.

The elevator dinged softly, a sound too mundane for the tension that filled the air as we stepped onto the fourth floor. The atmosphere changed perceptibly—colder, somehow heavier, as if the very air pressed against us, laden with unseen burdens.

Sarah led the way, her steps hesitant. She was a plain-spoken woman, that I knew intuitively. She wasn't comfortable with what was happening here and didn't really want to talk about it, but her business was on the line.

"This is where I saw the face," she whispered, stopping near a large window that offered a panoramic view of the city below. The idea that someone, or something, could be peering from such a height was unsettling.

I moved closer, my hand reaching out to the cool glass, half expecting to feel an electric charge of paranormal energy. I felt nothing but that did not mean I didn't believe her. Ghosts, entities, in general enjoyed playing games. Either that or having an energy source was truly necessary for manifestation.

Midas stood beside me, the recorder in his hand now, capturing every word, every pause in Sarah's story. "And Gianna?" he asked gently, prompting her to continue.

"She saw him first, actually. Right here," Sarah pointed to a spot just to the left of where we stood. "She said he was staring at her, his eyes... she said his eyes were empty, hollow. I feel so ashamed. I didn't believe her. Not at first but you know what they say. Seeing is believing. I sure as heck believe now."

A chill ran down my spine, the psychic in me reacting to the hidden layers of Sarah's account. There was more here, a story untold, a history unseen.

I glanced out the window and studied Mobile, half expecting to see a face staring back. The city sprawled oblivious below us, a stark contrast to the silent scream that seemed to echo through the empty apartment.

"So nobody lives in this apartment?" Midas asked Cal. "I don't see much in the way of personal items."

"No. I can't keep a resident. I guess we know why. I guess. What could that face be about? Do you think it was a trick of the light? I need something, Midas. Something to make my residents comfortable. And Sarah. She's like a daughter to me."

Before they could describe more about the scary incident, the temperature in the room dropped suddenly. Our breaths turned to mist in the air, a physical manifestation of the spectral presence we were here to confront. I could feel the hairs on the back of my neck stand on end, a sure sign that we were not alone.

Midas glanced at me and I immediately dug in my backpack for my temperature reader. Oh yeah. It was seventy-five degrees outside, but in the building, it was sixty six degrees and getting colder by the second. Sarah touched Cal's shoulder and he patted her hand.

Yes, we were all feeling something. "Oh no," I didn't mean to say that, but the temperature continued to drop to six six, point six. "We have a prankster."

Then, as if to confirm our worst suspicions, a soft thud echoed from the hallway outside. We all turned simultaneously, a collective intake of breath marking the moment. Midas signaled for us to stay put, his protective nature taking over as he stepped into the hallway to investigate.

The seconds stretched into eternity as we waited, the silence oppressive. When Midas returned, his expression was grim. "There's nothing there," he said, "but it felt like... like someone was watching."

Sarah nodded, her eyes wide with fear. "It's always like this these days," she murmured. "You feel them before you see them. And sometimes, you never see them at all, but they're here, watching, waiting."

-"When did all this start, Cal? Sarah? Have there been any renovations? Any seances? Anything obvious?" Midas was eager to get answers but it wasn't going to be that easy. Nobody seemed to have any idea how this started.

The words hung in the air between us, a stark reminder of the invisible world that brushed against ours, unseen but deeply felt. As we made our way back to the elevator, the weight of the tower's secrets bore down on us, a silent testament to the stories etched into its walls, waiting to be uncovered.

Once we were back in the car, the air between Midas and me was thick with unspoken thoughts. We sat in silence for a moment, letting the events of the tower settle around us like dust.

Finally, Midas broke the silence, his voice a low rumble. "We need to get ahead of this but the research is going to be tough," he said, pulling out his notebook and beginning to scribble down some initial thoughts.

I nodded, pulling out my own notes. "Equipment-wise, we're going to need everything. Cameras, voice recorders, EMF meters... and I think we should set up a static camera on the fourth floor, where Sarah saw the face."

The words came out in a rush, my brain already ticking through logistics and possibilities. "Yeah, but the sound in the hall?" Midas met my gaze, his expression serious. "Good idea though. And we'll need to do historical research on the property. There might be clues in the past that could help us understand what's happening now."

"Yeah, and we need more interviews," I added, thinking about the residents Sarah and Cal mentioned. "We should talk to the other employees, maybe some of the seniors living on the lower floors. Anyone who might have experienced something similar. Definitely Gianni, if she'll agree to meet with us. I get the feeling that Sarah is protecting her."

We spent the ride back to the Gulf Coast Paranormal office outlining our plan of action, each suggestion a piece of the puzzle we were about to dive into.

Despite the looming challenge, a part of me buzzed with the adrenaline of the hunt. This was why we did what we did, after all—to seek answers in the shadows, to bring light to the darkest of places.

Okay, I'm a thrill seeker. I would never admit it aloud, especially not to my husband, Joshua. I call him that all the time.

As the tower faded into the distance behind us, I found myself lost in thought, replaying the day's events over in my mind. The fear in Sarah's eyes, the chill of the fourth floor, the unexplained thud... it all swirled together into a haunting melody that I couldn't shake.

My role at Gulf Coast Paranormal had always been a mixture of skeptic and believer, grounded in the tangible but open to the mysteries of the unseen. Or so I liked to tell myself. I was sure that was hugely inaccurate.

Today had tilted the scales again.

Feeling the presence in the tower, experiencing the drop in temperature firsthand... it was a stark reminder of the realities we often faced but rarely got used to. At least, I didn't get used to them.

The mix of excitement and trepidation was a familiar cocktail, one that I sipped slowly as we drove away from the tower. What lay ahead was unknown, a path shrouded in mist and mystery.

Once we were a safe distance away, Midas made the call to the rest of the team. The speakerphone filled the car with the sounds of our team's voices, each one a reminder of the family we'd built within the walls of Gulf Coast Paranormal.

"We should be there in fifteen. Thanks for waiting around, guys. We've got a big case. It's legit. I'd bet the farm on it," Midas started, his voice firm. He recapped the day's findings, not missing a beat. As he spoke, I watched the sun dip lower in the sky, casting long shadows across the road.

The team's reactions were a mix of concern, curiosity, and determination. Cassidy's voice was the last to chime in, her tone steady. "Drive safe. We will see you in a few minutes. Let's figure this out, together."

Hanging up the phone, I felt a surge of gratitude for our little band of investigators.

Whatever awaited us at the RSA Battle House Tower, we wouldn't face it alone. The investigation was just beginning, and together, we would peel back the layers of mystery that shrouded the tower and presumably the land it sat upon. I had an inkling that property had something to do with the disturbance.

I couldn't help but feel a sense of purpose light up within me.

The road ahead was uncertain, fraught with shadows and whispers, but we were Gulf Coast Paranormal.

We faced the unknown head-on, and this time would be no different.

It was game on.

Chapter Three–Midas

The drive back from the Gulf Coast Paranormal office left me alone with my thoughts, the hum of the engine a quiet backdrop to the replay of today's meeting. Cassidy had taken Dominic to grab our dinner, leaving me to navigate the quiet streets bathed in the golden hues of the setting sun.

Sierra's words from earlier lingered in my mind, a mix of concern and unwavering determination that mirrored my own feelings about the towering challenge ahead. The RSA Tower, with its thirty five floors and an intimidating array of fourteen elevators, seemed like a daunting adversary.

"How are we going to cover it all?" I found myself whispering to the empty passenger seat beside me, the question echoing in the confined space of my car. It felt like speaking it aloud gave the challenge a form, making it more real and pressing.

"Sleep on it," Sierra had suggested earlier, her smile a beacon of optimism in the shadow of our task. "We'll stick to the lower four floors," I had agreed with her, though the words were more for my own benefit than anyone else's. "It's not like we have to investigate the whole thing at once," I reasoned, trying to convince myself as much as her.

Pulling into the driveway, the familiar sight of home offered a semblance of normalcy after a day filled with the supernatural. Yet, the weight of our upcoming investigation into the RSA Tower's mysteries refused to be left at the door, following me inside like a persistent shadow.

Stepping through the door, the immediate sense of home wrapped around me, a stark contrast to the looming uncertainty of the tower. The smell of baked calzones, rich with tomato and oregano, filled the air, a comforting reminder of normalcy.

Yet, the house was quieter than expected; Cassidy and Dominic weren't in their usual spot to greet me. The absence of their presence added a layer of stillness that seemed out of place.

I wandered down the hallway, the day's events replayed in my mind like a looped recording. The tower, with its myriad of floors and hidden secrets, cast a long shadow over my thoughts.

Cassidy's laughter from earlier and Sierra's determined words mingled in my memory, a blend of light and resolve against the backdrop of our challenge.

The aroma led me to the kitchen, where I found the calzones resting on the table, their warmth seeping into the cool air of the room. But it was the lack of noise that drew my attention—no babbling from Dominic, no soft humming from Cassidy. It was an unusual quiet, one that felt heavy with anticipation.

A sudden shout broke the silence, putting a smile onto my face despite the whirlwind of thoughts. Dominic's voice, echoed from the direction of the art studio. It was a sound that grounded me, a reminder of what was important amidst the chaos of our work.

Following the sounds, I found myself moving towards Cassidy's art studio, the heart of creativity in our home—even though it was a converted garage behind the house.

The prospect of seeing them both, enveloped in the warm glow of familial love, offered a brief respite from the spectral shadows that lingered at the back of my mind.

As I pushed open the door to Cassidy's art studio, the shift from the quiet of the house to the creativity-infused chaos was immediate. Canvases littered the space, each one a testament to Cassidy's talent and the way she saw the world. Bright sunlight filtered through the windows, casting everything in a warm, inviting glow.

Yet, it was a specific piece that captured my attention and held it, transforming the room's warmth into a cold, uneasy feeling.

There, amidst the riot of colors and bold strokes that characterized Cassidy's work, was a painting that seemed out of place.

It depicted Sarah, her eyes wide with a mix of fear and disbelief. Behind her, almost blending into the shadows, a shadowy figure loomed—a terrifying entity that seemed to gaze right out of the canvas, its presence unsettlingly palpable.

"Daddy!"

Dominic's exuberant yell cut through my fixation on the painting. I turned to see him barreling towards me, a blur of energy and joy. Scooping him up into my arms, I planted a smooch on his cheek, his laughter a balm to the eerie disturbance the painting had stirred in me. He was growing up so fast, each day bringing new words, new discoveries.

Holding him close, I was reminded of the world beyond our investigations—a world filled with light, love, and the innocence of childhood.

Yet, as Dominic babbled on about his day, my gaze was drawn back to the painting. Cassidy had somehow captured the essence of our investigation, the palpable fear and the unknown threat we were about to face. It was a stark reminder of the reality that lay behind our work, the reasons why we did what we did.

"Looks like Mommy's been busy," I remarked, trying to keep my voice light despite the unease that Cassidy's art had sparked within me. Dominic, oblivious to the undercurrents of our adult concerns, simply leaned back to look at me, his smile wide and untroubled. I kissed my wife's paint streaked cheek.

Cassidy, noticing where my attention had landed, wiped her hands on her apron and joined us. "It came to me in a day dream," she explained, her voice tinged with a seriousness that matched the painting's mood. "I had to get it on canvas. Uh...you recognize her?"

The studio, usually a place of inspiration and warmth, felt different now, the painting casting a long shadow over the space. It was a physical manifestation of the case that awaited us, a silent warning of the darkness we were stepping into.

Holding Dominic closer, I realized that this investigation was not just another case. It was personal, and the stakes were higher than ever.

Cassidy's brush had unwittingly drawn a line in the sand with that painting. As Dominic nestled into my arms, his energy momentarily subdued as he sensed the shift in mood, I couldn't tear my eyes away from the canvas. The depicted fear, the looming threat behind Sarah—it was more than just art. It was a call to action.

"Yeah, that's one of the people I met today. Her name is Sarah. I can't believe this, but then again," I finally spoke, my voice a mix of awe and resolve. Cassidy, leaning against the worktable, watched me closely, her green eyes reflecting the seriousness of our conversation. The shadowy man standing behind Sarah sickened me.

"This... This is exactly what we're up against. It's like you've seen into the heart of the tower's mystery."

Cassidy shrugged, a modest tilt of her head, her red hair catching the light. "I just paint what I see, Midas. I'm glad if this helps you see what needs to be done..." Her voice trailed off, leaving the sentence hanging, unfinished yet clear.

Dominic, picking up on the intensity of the moment, quieted, his small hand reaching out to touch the painting as if understanding its importance.

"No touch, buddy," I gently reprimanded, shifting him in my arms so he couldn't reach the canvas. "This... this painting is why we do what we do. It's more than just chasing shadows. It's about facing down these nightmares."

Cassidy nodded, her expression softening. "So, we're investigating the RSA Tower. Wow."

"Yes," I confirmed, my decision firmer now than ever. "We have to help Sarah and Gianna... and anyone else caught in this thing. Cassidy, this painting—it's a reminder of what's at stake."

Dominic, sensing the mood lightening, began to squirm, reaching for Cassidy. I handed him over, watching as she embraced our son, her presence a comforting counterbalance to the eerie foreboding of her own creation.

"Let's do it right," I added, my gaze shifting between Cassidy and the painting. "We start first thing tomorrow. I'll call Sierra and the team tonight. Let's get lots of photos of your work and make sure we send them out via text. We'll need all hands on deck for this one. I sure hope Chris joins us but I know I shouldn't push him."

"I agree, honey. I don't think he's ready. Yes, he's been cleared, but he is dealing with a lot of guilt. I can't shake the feeling that there's more to the story. Who knows. I sure don't. Whatever you decide, I'm down." Dominic made sure he got paint on his hands. "Son!" Cassidy laughed as she hurriedly handed him back to me and grabbed a warm, damp cloth to erase the paint.

"We're only focusing on the lower four floors. There are no reports of paranormal activity anywhere else. It's just something in the senior residential area."

Cassidy smiled, the warrior spirit I'd fallen in love with shining through. "We've got this," she said confidently, echoing the sentiment with a conviction that bolstered my own.

As I left the studio, Dominic's laughter echoing behind me, the weight of our task felt a little lighter. Cassidy's painting bridged the gap between our daily lives and the unseen world we were about to confront.

The decision was made. The Gulf Coast Paranormal team would face the tower's darkness head-on, and somehow, I knew we were exactly where we needed to be.

My phone buzzed to life, breaking the momentary silence. It was Cal, his voice on the line sounding both anxious and relieved to have us on board. "Midas, I've arranged for you to have access to the apartment where Sarah saw... whatever it is she saw," he began, the gravity of the situation clear in his tone.

I sat up, rubbing my tired eyes. I haven't been sleeping great lately. I was always tired. My mind immediately shifting into investigative mode. "That's great news, Cal. Access to that apartment could be crucial for us." The prospect of exploring the site of the initial sighting firsthand offered a tangible starting point, something solid in the midst of all the unknowns.

Cal's next words were spoken in a lower tone, as if sharing a secret. "Listen, if anyone asks, you're just there investigating a supposed piping issue. We need to keep this under wraps, not just for the tower's reputation, but to avoid causing panic among the residents."

I understood the need for discretion all too well. "Of course, Cal. Discretion is part of the job," I assured him, my mind already ticking through the logistics of maintaining such a cover. "The less people that know about the real reason we're there, the smoother this will go."

"There's more," Cal continued, his voice tinged with a seriousness that demanded full attention. "I've asked the residents of the affected floors to temporarily relocate. They think it's for the piping work, but it's really so you can investigate without interference. The apartments will be empty, and you won't have to worry about running into anyone."

A sense of relief washed over me. Having the space to investigate without the added complexity of navigating around the tower's residents was a blessing. "That's incredibly helpful, Cal. Thank you for setting this up. It'll give us the freedom to conduct a thorough investigation."

"We're all counting on you, Midas. Just... be careful, alright? I don't know what's in there, but I knew this cleaning crew. They aren't scared of hard work. They wouldn't make this up. I believe them and I too...well, it doesn't feel right here. Especially at night."

His words sent a shiver down my spine, a reminder of the seriousness of what we were about to undertake. "We will be, Cal. You have my word. We'll get to the bottom of this," I responded, the resolve in my voice firm.

Hanging up, I stared out the window at lightning striking across the sky, the conversation with Cal replaying in my mind. We needed the rain but I wasn't a huge fan of thunderstorms.

The night was upon us, bringing with it the promise of rest and hopefully, tomorrow a resolution to the haunting that plagued the RSA Tower. The path forward was clear, but the shadows that awaited us were anything but.

That night, the house was enveloped in a deceptive calm, a quiet that felt eerily like the stillness that precedes a tempest.

Domino, our mischievous black cat, broke the silence now and then, his playful antics with Dominic a welcome distraction. Yet, even his sudden pounces at my ankles, which usually elicited a laugh, couldn't fully penetrate the preoccupation that clouded my thoughts. Cassidy must have sensed my apprehension—or whatever this was; she squeezed my hand and kissed me briefly to let me know she cared.

I found myself repeatedly glancing at Cassidy's painting, which we had decided to leave leaning against the wall in the living room. The paint was dry and thankfully, our son was no longer interested in drawing on it. Its presence was both unsettling and compelling, drawing my attention away from the family movie night we attempted to immerse ourselves in. Cassidy noticed my distraction but chose not to comment, understanding the weight of what lay ahead.

Later, as the house settled into the deeper quiet of the night, and Cassidy and Dominic were sound asleep, I found myself wide awake.

Restlessness tugged at me, urging me out of bed. I padded softly through the darkened house, drawn as if by a magnetic pull to the painting that had captivated my attention earlier.

Standing before it in the dim light, the eerie sense of being watched washed over me. The entity in the painting, with its undefined features lurking behind Sarah, seemed almost alive, its gaze piercing beyond the canvas.

I studied the face, the malevolent aura it exuded, searching for any clue, any detail that might give us an advantage in the investigation. The unknown aspects of what we were about to face loomed large, casting long shadows over my thoughts.

The stillness of the house contrasted sharply with the storm of emotions and questions swirling within me. It was a moment of introspection, of steeling myself for what was to come. The painting, a vivid representation of the fear and unknown we were about to confront, served as a silent sentinel, a reminder of the reality of our work.

The night might be quiet, but it was indeed calm before the storm. Tomorrow, we would step into the heart of the mystery, into the depths of the RSA Tower. The painting would be our beacon, a guide through the darkness we were determined to illuminate.

Cassidy's soft footsteps approached, her voice cutting through the silence, tinged with worry. "Midas, come back to bed," she urged, her voice a gentle beacon in the night.

I turned to her, the shadows playing across her features, highlighting the concern in her eyes. The tension in my body began to ease at her touch, her presence a reminder of the normalcy and warmth waiting for me beyond the reach of our work.

As we settled back into bed, her arms wrapped around me, providing a comfort that I had been missing since we took on this case. The familiarity of her embrace, the scent of her hair, it all brought me back from the edge of the abyss that our work often skirted.

For a moment, lost in each other, the world outside, with all its mysteries and shadows, faded away. "Cassidy, do you know how much I love you?"

"Yes, I do. I love you too. Now, show me how much you want me," she grinned mischievously, her suggestion clear. She didn't have to ask me twice.

Yet, as the adrenaline of our passionate session waned, my mind couldn't help but drift back to the task at hand. Sierra's unwavering determination, Cassidy's contribution through her art, the unity and strength of our team—these thoughts filled me with a mix of pride and resolve.

Despite the size of our group, there was a resilience among us, a shared commitment to shed light on the darkest corners of the world.

Lying there, with Cassidy's steady breathing beside me, the events of the day began to replay in my mind. Each moment, from the drive back from the office to the haunting image of the painting, was a step closer to understanding the depth of the mystery we faced. Yet, it was the collective spirit of our team, our combined efforts and talents, that truly gave me hope. We were more than just investigators; we were a family, bound by a common goal and driven by a shared desire to make a difference.

The tower, with all its secrets and unseen threats, loomed large in my thoughts. But so too did the image of us coming together, each playing our part in the unfolding drama. The challenges ahead were daunting, but not insurmountable. Not with Sierra's resolve, Cassidy's insight, and the support of the entire Gulf Coast Paranormal team.

As sleep finally began to claim me, a sense of peace settled over my thoughts. The night's quiet, once a haunting precursor to the storm, now felt like a momentary respite, a chance to gather strength for the day ahead.

Tomorrow, we would begin our investigation in earnest, stepping into the unknown with open eyes and hearts ready to face whatever awaited us. Our team was small, but our resolve was mighty, and together, we were ready for whatever the tower held.

Or at least that's what I told myself.

Chapter Four–Sierra

The night had wrapped our home in its quiet embrace, a stillness so profound it felt like the world outside had ceased to exist. Occasionally, a blue flash of lightning brightened the bedroom, but the rain never arrived.

This tranquility, however, was shattered in an instant. Bozo, our bulldog who was more accustomed to lounging on his back than actually standing guard, burst into a frenzied barking. His sudden alarm was like a siren in the silence, piercing the veil of sleep and catapulting me into wakefulness. Bozo's bark was deep and persistent.

Joshua, ever the deep sleeper, stirred next to me, his voice groggy and laced with concern. "You okay?" he mumbled, the words barely escaping the confines of his drowsiness. "Is he okay? What's up with him?"

"He's probably barking at the lightning. He's not a fan," I responded, my voice a mere whisper in the darkness. My heart pounded, not just from the abrupt awakening, but from something else—a sensation that something was amiss.

It wasn't just Bozo's barking; it was as if the air itself had shifted, charged with an unseen presence. Despite Bozo quieting down, the feeling of unease didn't dissipate, hanging heavy in the room like a dense fog.

There was something here with us, an energy I couldn't decipher as friendly or malevolent. It left me on edge, skin prickling with a cold that had nothing to do with the night air.

The fragile silence of the night was once again torn asunder, not by Bozo this time, but by a sound far more distressing—the cry of our daughter, Emily, piercing through the static tension that filled the house. It was a sharp, urgent sound, one that cut straight to the heart, driving away any remnants of sleep that lingered.

Joshua's concern deepened, mirroring my own as he turned towards me, the shadows playing across his face. "Should I...?" he began, already starting to rise, his instincts as a father kicking in.

"No, I've got her," I whispered, pressing a hand against his chest to gently ease him back down. "You stay. I'll go check on Emily. Maybe check on Bozo though." Pulling the covers aside, I swung my legs out of bed, the cool air of the room wrapping around me like a chilly embrace.

The walk to Emily's room felt longer than usual, each step propelled by a mixture of apprehension and the maternal need to comfort.

Why did it feel as if I were walking through gelatin?

As I moved through the dimly lit hallway, illuminated only by the intermittent flashes of lightning, the feeling of being watched grew stronger. It was an unsettling sensation, one that seemed to follow me, closing in with each step I took towards my daughter's room.

Reaching her door, I paused for a moment, taking a deep breath to steady my nerves. Her crying had ceased, leaving behind a heavy silence that seemed to press down on me from all sides. Even Bozo had gone quiet.

With a mother's resolve, I pushed the door open. Stepping into the room, prepared to change her wet pull ups, Emily couldn't seem to get the hang of potty training, I was surprised to see she was fast asleep. I couldn't count how many times I had to change her clothes and bedding in the middle of the night.

I shivered as I tucked the quilt around her. The warmth that usually enveloped the space was absent, replaced by an inexplicable chill that made me shiver. The playful pink walls and scattered toys created a stark contrast to the coldness that now filled the air.

Hadn't we cleaned all this up earlier? I didn't think too much about it, Em had a habit of getting up to play even when she was supposed to go to sleep. As I moved closer to her bed, my attention was abruptly diverted.

There, by the sliding closet door, materialized a woman, her form etched with the unmistakable silhouette of the 1700s. The ghostly light from the window cast her in a haunting pallor, illuminating the intricate details of her attire—a dress that whispered tales of a bygone era, each fold and stitch a testament to a time long past.

Our eyes locked, and time itself seemed to halt, suspending us in a moment that was as surreal as it was terrifying. At least her eyes weren't black—or red, which was entirely horrible.

Her gaze pierced through the dimness of the room, carrying with it an eerie sense of recognition, as if her soul had known mine across centuries.

The air around me thickened with the weight of her unspoken story, her presence as palpable as the chilling draft that now danced upon my skin. In the silence of that encounter, her eyes spoke volumes, a spectral bridge connecting her world to mine, filled with secrets from an age where shadows reigned and whispers spoke of fates untold.

The silence was deafening—at first, the only sound was my own heartbeat echoing in my ears.

Child, hold the child.

Then, as if compelled by a force unseen, the woman began to move, her form gliding effortlessly towards Emily's bed.

Panic surged within me. "No!" The word tore from my throat, a desperate plea, as I lunged forward to protect my child. "Leave her alone!"

But as I reached the bed, my hands grasped at nothing. The woman, the apparition that had stood so clearly before me, had vanished into thin air, leaving no trace behind.

Emily's bedroom felt empty, colder than before, a void where the spirit's presence had once been. My heart raced, not just from the rush of movement, but from the realization that what I had witnessed was beyond the realm of the normal.

Yes, she had been here, this ghost from another era, her attention fixed on Emily.

The implications of her visitation were as chilling as the air that now seemed to seep into my bones.

Joshua, roused by the sharpness of my cry, arrived at the doorway just as I was reeling from the apparition's disappearance. His hand landed lightly on my shoulder, an attempt to comfort, but in my heightened state, it felt like a bolt of electricity, causing me to whirl around in startled panic.

The stark fear in my gaze met his, a silent scream for understanding.

"I saw a ghost," I gasped out, the confession spilling from me in a torrent of words, "Right here, in Emily's room." My eyes darted back to our daughter's peaceful form, nestled snugly under her blankets. The serenity of her sleep was a stark contrast to the tumult in my heart.

Did her cry even herald this encounter, or had something more sinister mimicked her voice to lure me here?

Joshua's expression shifted from concern to a resolve as he processed my words. "I'll stay with Emily tonight," he declared firmly, moving towards our daughter's bed with a protective stance. His decision to keep watch over her for the remainder of the night was both a reassurance and a testament to the unsettling nature of what had just occurred.

As he settled in, a makeshift guardian against unseen forces, the surrealism of our situation hung heavily in the room. I covered them both with a larger quilt. I kissed him and then touched Emily's cheek carefully without waking her up.

The normalcy of our family life had been breached by something beyond our understanding, leaving us grappling with the reality of our encounter.

I lingered at the doorway for a moment longer, torn between the desire to stay and the need to distance myself from the site of such unearthly visitation.

Turning back to the quiet of the house, the questions and fears multiplied with each step I took away from Emily's room. The encounter with the ghost, her warning—or was it a plea—echoed in my mind, a haunting melody that refused to be silenced.

Retreating to the solitude of our bedroom, the ghostly visage of the woman lingered at the forefront of my mind, her spectral presence a sharp contrast to the mundane safety of my surroundings.

This encounter was no random haunting—I wasn't a fool. And this wasn't the first time a spirit from an investigation had invaded my home.

No, this visit bore a direct connection to the mysteries we were probing into. The weight of this realization pressed down on me, intertwining fear with a resolute determination to unearth the truth behind her appearance.

Settling back into the bed that suddenly felt too large and too empty, I wrapped myself in the blankets, seeking comfort in their familiar embrace. Yet, comfort remained just out of reach. The night, once a blanket of peace, now felt like a thin veil barely separating me from a realm of unsettled spirits and unfinished stories.

The image of the woman, so clear and so charged with an ancient sorrow, haunted the edges of my consciousness. *Was her visitation a warning, a plea, or perhaps a clue unwittingly delivered from the past?* The air in the room felt charged, as if her presence had left a trace of her essence behind, a whisper of her existence that lingered in the spaces between shadows.

As sleep began to reclaim me, a soft, sorrowful weeping seemed to drift through the silence of the house. My heart ached for the strange spirit bound by a grief that had transcended time.

Yet, as the ethereal sound wove through my drowsy thoughts, a protective instinct surged within me—a reminder that, whatever her reasons, my first duty was to the safety and peace of my living family.

Especially my baby girl. No way was a ghost going to mess with her. Not if I had breath in my body.

Yes, something tragic had befallen the spirit, tethering her to our world with chains of sorrow. But her presence in Emily's room was a boundary crossed, a line that blurred the realms of the living and the dead.

As the shadows danced in the faint light, the soft weeping continued, a ghostly lullaby that was both haunting and heartrending.

In the liminal space between wakefulness and sleep, I resolved to find answers, not just for the sake of our investigation, but for her as well. If there was peace to be offered to a soul so clearly tormented, then I would strive to find it, not only to protect my family but to give rest to a spirit caught in the throes of an eternal grief.

The darkness of my bedroom dissolved into the murky depths of a bygone era, and I found myself no longer lying in the safety of my bed but running, breath ragged, through a swamp thick with the hum of mosquitoes.

Each step was a desperate bid for survival, the cold mud clinging to my skirts as if the very earth itself sought to claim me.

My name was Helene.

The realization hit me with the force of a physical blow, disorienting in its intensity.

I wasn't merely dreaming; I was living through her eyes, feeling her fear as acutely as if it were my own. The night air was heavy with the scent of decay and water, and the sounds of pursuit were a constant terror at my back. I was crying so hard I could barely see.

Around me, the swamp was alive with unseen dangers, but none as immediate or as deadly as the ones from which I fled.

The echo of my pursuers' shouts mingled with the croak of frogs and the occasional splash of water, painting a soundscape of dread that urged me onward, despite my exhaustion. *Francis had again let me down. Again, failed to protect me, protect our child!*

My heart pounded in my chest, a wild rhythm that matched the frenetic pace of my flight. Every shadow seemed to hide a threat, every sound a warning. Yet, amidst the fear, there was a burning indignation, a sense of injustice that fueled my determination to escape the fate that my accusers sought to impose upon me.

Where can I go? Where do I go?

As I ran, the boundary between Helene's time and my own blurred, her memories becoming mine.

I could feel the despair, the betrayal, but also the fierce will to live, to prove her innocence against the false accusations that had turned her world into a nightmare.

The swamp stretched on, endless and unforgiving, but Helene's spirit refused to break.

And as I raced through the darkness, her resolve became my own, a shared determination to survive the night and to uncover the truth that had been buried in the murky waters of the past.

The next morning, I woke drenched in sweat and when I pulled the covers back, I screamed. My bare feet were covered in mud. I was still screaming when Joshua and Emily ran into the room.

I cried until I could cry no more.

Chapter Five–Midas

The early evening air was crisp, a harbinger of the coming false fall, as we gathered in the shadow of the RSA Battle House Tower. The team, our tight-knit group bound by countless investigations, stood before the modern monolith, its glass facade reflecting the last rays of the setting sun. We had decided against arriving in our official Gulf Coast Paranormal van, opting instead for discretion given the sensitivity and potential scope of this case.

I took a moment to scan the faces of my team—Sierra, Joshua, Cassidy, Macie, and Jericho. Each carried a mix of determination and the underlying tension that always accompanied the start of a new investigation.

Chris was notably absent, his recent experiences leaving him in need of a break from the field. I felt his absence keenly, a reminder of the personal costs these investigations sometimes exacted.

"We know the plan," I started, my voice low but firm. "But let's remember to be thorough and cautious. We don't know what we're walking into." Nods of agreement met my words, a silent testament to the trust and respect among us.

Macie, our resident hippy, kind of like her late sister Jocelyn, hefted her bag of equipment, a small smile playing on her lips. "Trippy," she murmured, her gaze lifting to the towering structure above us. It was her way of acknowledging the blend of excitement and uncertainty that always tinged our initial steps into the unknown. I could see it on her face, she was ready to get in there and do some automatic writing.

We made our way inside, the lobby's modernity a stark contrast to the age-old phenomena we were here to investigate. The air inside felt charged, as if the building itself was aware of our intentions.

Gathering our gear from the unmarked vehicles, we prepared to confront whatever secrets lay hidden within the RSA Battle House Tower's walls. Cassidy handed out the EMF meters and digital recorders, while Jericho checked the batteries on the night vision cameras. Our arsenal of equipment was the latest the field had to offer, but against the unseen, one could never be too prepared.

And batteries? I went nowhere without tons of extra batteries.

Inside the RSA Battle House Tower, the air felt heavy, as if laden with whispered secrets and unseen eyes watching our every move. The lobby, vast and echoing with our footsteps, was dimly lit by the fading daylight that struggled through the glass facade. The modernity of the building did little to dispel the ancient energy that seemed to seep through its walls.

"Let's get baseline readings, guys," Macie suggested, unzipping her bag to pull out an EMF meter. Cassidy nodded in agreement, powering on her digital recorder, the red light blinking into life in the dimness.

Jericho and Joshua, meanwhile, began setting up the first of the night vision cameras at strategic points around the lobby. "This place is massive," Joshua commented, his voice low but it echoed quite loudly. "Makes you wonder what's hiding in all these shadows."

The empty space around us felt oppressive, a tangible reminder of the silence and darkness that dominated the building. Only the emergency lights provided some relief from the creeping shadows, casting an eerie glow that did little to warm the cold ambiance.

Macie held up her EMF meter, her brow furrowed in concentration as she scanned the area. "Nothing out of the ordinary yet," she announced, though the anticipation in her voice was clear. Cassidy, her recorder in hand, moved silently beside her, her eyes scanning the lobby with an experienced gaze. She glanced at the EMF reader in her other hand.

"Nothing here either," she confirmed softly.

"After we finish setting up the hallway cameras, let's head to the second floor," I decided, glancing at the group. A nod from each confirmed the decision, and we made our way to the elevator, the doors sliding open with a whisper that seemed too loud in the silence.

As the elevator ascended, the feeling of being watched intensified, a psychological pressure that was almost suffocating. The digital display ticked off the floors until the doors reopened, revealing the long, empty hallway of the second floor.

The only illumination came from the sparse emergency lights, their dim glow casting long shadows that seemed to stretch and twist in the corners of our vision.

"Guys? How are the elevators working if the lights are out? I mean, shouldn't all the power be out?"

"Yeah, that's weird. I mean I am glad we're climbing up flights of steps but yeah, it's weird. Feels like we're not alone," Cassidy whispered in a sing-songy manner, her voice barely above a breath. The comment sent a shiver down my spine, the truth of her words resonating with the tension that filled the air.

"Definitely, trippy," Macie added as she hiked her heavy backpack up on her shoulder.

Jericho and Joshua quickly set to work, placing cameras along the hallway on the second floor, their movements efficient but wary. The silence was oppressive, the only sound was our own breathing and the soft clicks of the equipment. These were wireless, motion activated cameras with night vision.

I pulled out my phone, intending to call Cal about the lack of power. "I agree. Strange for the lights to be out but the power seems to be working for the elevators," I murmured, dialing his number. The call went straight to voicemail, a dead end that added another layer of unease to the atmosphere. "Must be a power surge," I reasoned aloud, trying to dispel the growing tension.

"Good thing we brought our own power supply packs for the station setup on the fourth floor." Cassidy's attempt at reassurance was met with tight smiles, the underlying nervousness a shared sentiment among us. "I mean, we usually do investigate in the dark anyway."

The second floor was as silent and desolate as the first, a ghostly shell that whispered of secrets and stories left untold. We moved through it with a sense of purpose, our equipment a lifeline in the tangible darkness that seemed to press in from all sides.

As we prepared to ascend to the next floor, the sense of anticipation was palpable. Each floor promised new discoveries, each shadow a potential clue in the unfolding mystery of the RSA Battle House Tower.

Yet, the higher we ventured, the more we felt the weight of the unknown that awaited us, a silent specter that danced just out of reach in the darkness.

The elevator's soft ding signaled our arrival on the third floor, a silent herald into yet another dimly lit corridor. This level felt different, the air charged with an almost palpable anticipation of the unknown.

As we stepped out of the elevator, the muted echo of our footsteps seemed louder, more pronounced against the backdrop of the oppressive silence that greeted us. It was then we encountered the man—clearly, a peculiar resident who seemed oddly out of place amidst the modernity of the tower.

He was an old man, his back slightly hunched, eyes sharp and piercing as they locked onto ours. There was a knowing look in those eyes, a depth that spoke of secrets and truths hidden away from the light.

"Are you responsible for the lights going out?" he asked in a gravelly voice. "What are you doing here? I don't remember seeing you here before. I sure as hell didn't buzz you in."

"Midas," I reminded him gently, aware of the delicate situation, "everyone's supposed to be out of the building." To him, Sierra smiled sweetly, "There's a... piping issue."

The old man, who introduced himself as Hyram, scoffed at my explanation, a sound that seemed to echo down the long, empty hallway. "That's bull," he retorted, his voice a gravelly whisper that somehow carried the weight of years and knowledge. "There's nothing wrong with the pipes. Just the dang lights, at the moment. It's this place that's the problem. It's cursed. Don't believe me? Stick around."

Macie moved closer to Jericho, other than that none of us moved. I couldn't demand that he leave and thus far I hadn't been able to get Cal on the phone.

His words sent a shiver through the team, an involuntary reaction to the ominous tone of his warning. "I mean it! If you had any brains, you'd leave, before it's too late. This place is cursed!" Hyram continued, his gaze sweeping over each of us with a discerning eye.

The implication of his words, the hint of danger beyond our understanding, set a chilling precedent for the investigation. His presence, a stark reminder that the tower's mysteries were deeply intertwined with the lives of those who had called it home.

We exchanged uneasy glances, the weight of Hyram's cryptic warnings settling heavily upon us. There was a story here, a narrative woven into the very fabric of the RSA Battle House Tower, and Hyram, it seemed, might be a keyholder to its darkest chapters.

"Thank you, Hyram," I said, my voice steady despite the unease that his words had stirred. "We'll... keep that in mind."

But as we watched him shuffle away, disappearing into the shadows from whence he came, the reality of our task became ever more daunting. The tower, with all its secrets and silent cries, had just issued its first real warning, and we were right in the heart of it, teetering on the edge of a mystery that promised to be as terrifying as it was compelling.

The team gathered closer, the need for solidarity never more apparent. "Let's keep going," I urged, though my voice carried a hint of the trepidation we all felt. "We've got a job to do."

"Did anyone see which apartment he came from?" Sierra asked but nobody had an answer. "Should I go look?"

"No," Joshua objected. "Leave him alone. He gives me the creeps. Cursed. What the heck is he talking about?" And with that, we pressed on, each step taking us deeper into the heart of the tower's shadows, driven by a determination to uncover the truth, no matter how dark or unsettling it may prove to be. But I could tell Sierra wasn't satisfied with that idea.

Silence enveloped us for a moment, each of us lost in thought. "Well," Sierra finally broke the quiet, her voice a mixture of skepticism and concern, "that was... straight up weird."

I nodded, feeling the responsibility of our mission weighing heavily on me. "Let's keep our eyes open and stick together. Whatever this curse is he's talking about, we'll face it as a team." As we resumed our exploration, the echo of Hyram's warning lingered with us, a ghostly presence that seemed to whisper from the very walls of the tower.

As we moved deeper into the tower, Sierra suddenly halted, her expression one of intense concentration. The team stopped in unison, turning towards her, recognizing the familiar signs of her psychic senses at work.

"I sense... something," she whispered, her voice barely audible over the sound of our own breathing. "Despair, confusion... it's strong, coming from the walls themselves. There's a heavy presence here, especially on the fourth floor. Above us. I think Hyram really wanted to warn us." I glanced up at the ceiling.

Joshua put his hand on my arm which I resented. I didn't want to be interrupted. My husband had the worst timing at times. "I still think I should get his apartment number. He might have useful information, you know. Joshua, you're so superstitious."

Before we could digest Sierra's warning, my phone vibrated in my pocket, pulling our attention momentarily from the oppressive atmosphere. It was Cal, his voice tinged with concern.

"Midas, I got your message. I didn't turn out the lights. Are you sure you want to do this? I won't blame you if you want to walk away."

I shared a quick glance with the team, determination firm in their eyes. "Why would we do that? We're already in the building, Cal. But, by the way, one of your residents didn't leave. It's not a big deal. I don't think he believes the piping thing. Hyram? That's his name. Says he lives on the third floor. He thinks the place is cursed," I said, trying to inject some levity into the situation. "Strange old bird."

There was a pause on the other end, then Cal's voice, serious and a shade paler. "Midas, are you pulling my leg? There's no Hyram. Not anymore."

"What? What are you talking about? Hold on. Can I put you on speakerphone. Do you mind? I think the team should hear this."

"Hyram's been dead for six months, Midas. Hyram from the third floor, right? He fell down the stairs. God only knows why he didn't take the elevator. He was a kind of fitness nut."

A chill ran through the group at Cal's revelation, the air around us thickening with unspoken fears. Sierra's face paled, her earlier impressions suddenly cast in a more sinister light.

"Oh. Okay. Thanks for that information. Maybe we got it wrong. Maybe it was someone else. I'll call you later."

"Alright," Cal said but he didn't sound comforted or convinced.

"I tried to... reach out to him," Sierra said, her voice shaking slightly. "But he's being blocked by something else, something stronger."

The decision was made without words. We had to head to the fourth floor, our original target, but now with a heightened sense of urgency and caution.

The cameras and light sensors we set up along the way felt like breadcrumbs marking our path into an increasingly foreboding unknown.

That's when the elevators dinged. Even though none of us pressed the button. I glanced at Jericho and Joshua. They shook their heads to indicate a no answer. No, it wasn't them but the invitation was clear.

Whatever was about to go down, it was going down on the fourth floor. We carried the remaining gear with us and piled into the elevator together.

As the elevator doors closed behind us, sealing us off from the lower floors, we could all feel the weight of the tower's secrets pressing in around us.

Sierra's warning, Cal's unsettling news about Hyram, and the general heaviness that seemed to permeate the air created a cocktail of apprehension that accompanied us as we ascended.

The fourth floor awaited, silent and brooding, as if it held the key to the mysteries that wrapped the RSA Battle House Tower in whispers and shadows.

And we were stepping into the heart of the haunting, uncertain of what we might find or whether we were prepared for the truths hidden within its walls.

I don't know why I said this but when the door finally opened on the fourth floor I whispered. "Ready or not, here we come."

To my shock, I heard a male voice answer me.

Ready...

Chapter Six–Joshua

"Let's hope we caught that disembodied voice on one of our devices." I nodded in agreement. Disembodied voices were a rarity, for sure.

The hush of the fourth floor enveloped us as we began setting up our command center, what we affectionately call the "brain room," in the empty apartment we'd secured for the night's investigation. The room quickly transformed into the nerve center of our operation, filled with the soft glow of monitors, the tangle of cables, and the hum of electronic equipment powering on.

It was a familiar scene, one that always brought a sense of anticipation and, if I'm honest, a bit of apprehension. You can't always prepare for electronics that go bad or cords that somehow came unplugged.

Luckily, as we set up the monitors, the wireless cameras came online effortlessly.

I glanced around at the team, each person absorbed in their tasks, their faces lit by the blue light of screens, a stark contrast to the dim, shadow-filled spaces of the apartment.

Cassidy was meticulously examining each piece of equipment, while Macie and Jericho checked the digital recorders and EMF meters. Sierra was already tuning into the building's energy, her brow furrowed in concentration.

Yeah, I knew my wife. I knew all her expressions. At times, she went rogue but I loved her.

I had a secret tucked away in the van downstairs—the RYDER technology. It was a cutting-edge piece of equipment designed to detect and interact with spirit attachments, but after Chris's departure and the controversy surrounding its use, I'd decided to keep it under wraps for now.

I wasn't sure how the team, especially Sierra, would react to its presence, given its history and the raw nerves left in Chris's absence. And the fact that some people were gravely affected by its use.

So, I kept silent about RYDER, focusing instead on the task at hand. We were here to explore, to document, and, if we were lucky, to communicate with whatever resided within the RSA Battle House Tower. The brain room, with its banks of equipment, served as our anchor, a bastion of modern technology amidst the ancient energies we sought to understand.

As the final cables were connected and the last of the equipment buzzed to life, I took a moment to survey the brain room. It was a juxtaposition of the old and the new, a testament to our quest to pierce the veil between the living and the dead using the tools of the living.

The quiet in the "brain room" hung like a thick fog, broken only by the subtle, almost ghostly sounds of technology at work. The screens before us, aglow with the spectral images from the lower floors, cast our shadows long and twisted against the walls, creating a tableau that felt as if it were pulled from a nightmare.

Macie and Jericho, their heads close together in whispered consultation, seemed for a moment like figures from another age, plotting their next move in a game whose stakes were beyond the ken of ordinary understanding.

The air around us was charged, heavy with the anticipation of delving deep into the heart of mysteries that the RSA Battle House Tower had jealously guarded for ages.

As I prepared for the investigation, my heart was a drum of war in the quiet before the storm. The "brain room," now transformed into our command center, was alive with the silent whispers of the unseen, each piece of equipment a beacon in the darkness, seeking out the shadows that lurked just beyond our sight. And in the depths of my mind, the RYDER technology loomed—a silent specter, its potential both a promise and a threat to the veil that separated our world from the one that whispered to us from the corners of our fear.

The moment I laid eyes on the footage from the second floor, a chill crawled up my spine, freezing me in place.

"Holy crap!" I couldn't help but spit that out.

There, amidst the shadows and the eerie half-light, stood a figure so blatantly out of place, so profoundly disturbing, that it seemed to tear a hole in the fabric of reality itself.

Dressed in a black suit and top hat, the figure was a ghost from a bygone era, its eyes locked onto the camera with an intensity that felt almost personal, as if it saw not just the lens, but through it, into the very soul of the observer.

His stare was a weight, a palpable force that pressed against me, a cold hand reaching out from the past to grip my heart with fear.

Shit! He sees me!

"Guys! Anomaly on the second floor. Either that or someone broke in. The doors are locked, right?" Midas wasted no time checking out the screen. Everyone hung around the arrangement of monitors.

"Nope. It's locked. Seriously. Nobody's getting in here without the passcode and the key fob. Unless he was already here. Or he's something else."

"What's he doing?" Macie asked in almost a whimper. "He's staring at us. It's like he knows we can see him." As she spoke, the air in the room grew colder, the soft hum of our equipment now a distant echo as the figure in the top hat held us in thrall. The man's face was obscure, but I could feel his gaze and took it as a challenge.

The figure's stare was penetrating, its intensity suggesting an awareness, a consciousness that was far from benign.

"He's on the second floor, guys. Not outside the windows but inside the building," I explained, my voice tense with the implication of what we were witnessing.

Midas, ever the leader, didn't hesitate. "I'm going down," he announced with a determination that brooked no argument. But Cassidy, with a look of fierce resolve, quickly interjected, "Fat chance you're going by yourself. Come on." She grabbed her sketchbook and pencil bag, a testament to her readiness to document this encounter, alongside her electronic equipment.

Sierra hollered, "Hold on! Nobody leaves the room without a radio. Channel four, guys. Midas, take the handheld. We want to see everything."

Cassidy accepted the radio and checked the channel. Together, the pair would confront this apparition, this entity that had so boldly made its presence known. The figure in the top hat, so clearly captured on our cameras, was a significant piece of the puzzle, a clue to the mysteries that enshrouded the tower.

And then he was gone. "Shit! He vanished. Walked right out of the frame." I tapped the keyboard and accessed the opposite cameras but we couldn't see him any longer.

The entity's appearance and now disappearance, had changed the game, transforming our investigation into a direct confrontation with something that, until now, had remained hidden in the shadows. Or at least the reflection of window glass.

Midas tapped on the camera, and we quickly made a connection. I could see what he could see on the monitor. The rest of the team gathered around to watch over it.

The elevator ride down to the second floor was tense, I could feel it. Nobody had to say anything. Cassidy clutched her sketchbook close, her readiness to capture the encounter a silent vow to document and understand. Midas led the way, his resolve a steady beacon that guided us through the uncertainty that lay ahead.

From the monitor, the rest of us watched as the doors of the elevator slid open, revealing the darkened hallway where the figure had been seen, a palpable sense of anticipation filled the air.

With each step they took, the reality of our investigation took on a new dimension, one where the line between the living and the dead blurred, challenging our understanding of the world and our place within it. The night ahead promised revelations and, perhaps, confrontations with truths long buried beneath layers of time and silence.

As the hunt for the apparition's source began, skepticism and unease danced a tightrope in my mind. "There has to be a logical explanation," I murmured to myself, half in denial of the chilling reality displayed on our monitors.

Sierra tapped her radio. "You guys okay?"

"Sierra Kay, you can see them," I didn't mean to sound cranky and state the obvious but I was suddenly a nervous wreck. "So far, so good."

Midas radioed back. "Yep. All good. Going radio silent for now."

Midas and Cassidy, now our eyes and ears on the second floor, were on a mission to debunk the sighting of the figure in the top hat, searching for any hint of a hoax—a hidden projector or camera that might explain the unexplainable. Immediately I could see Cassidy pointing her flashlight high on the walls in search of projectors or other equipment. So far, there was nothing to see.

Their progress was a live feed in our makeshift command center, every step and turn broadcasted through the handheld radio Midas carried. After about fifteen minutes of searching up and down, they found no trace of the man in the suit. No trace of anyone.

"Checking the first apartment on this floor," Midas's voice crackled through the speaker, a hint of tension betraying his usual calm demeanor.

Cassidy's voice chimed in, a mix of determination and apprehension, "Door is locked. No signs of forced entry. What do you want to bet all of the apartments are locked?"

The team watched along with me, our collective breath held, as they moved from door to door, the dim emergency lighting casting long, eerie shadows that seemed to stretch and twist with a life of their own.

"Nothing here," Cassidy reported after inspecting another locked door, the disappointment and growing unease evident in her voice.

The logical part of me clung to the hope of finding a hidden device, a tangible piece of evidence to rationalize the chilling visage of the man in the top hat. Yet, as Midas and Cassidy's search yielded nothing but locked doors and empty hallways, the reality of our situation began to sink in. The absence of any logical explanation only served to deepen the mystery, a cold knot of fear settling in the pit of my stomach.

"They've checked every apartment," I announced to the rest of the team still with me, my voice betraying the sinking feeling of dread that had taken hold. "Every door is locked. There's nowhere he could have hidden."

The suggestion to check the bathrooms came as a last-ditch effort to cling to a shred of skepticism. "Heading to the bathrooms now," Midas confirmed, the determination in his voice a thin veneer over the growing realization that we were dealing with something far beyond our understanding. "Cassidy is taking the camera now."

The team watched in silence as Midas entered each bathroom, his flashlight cutting through the darkness, revealing nothing but the stark, mundane reality of tiled walls and mirrored surfaces. No hidden cameras, no projectors, nothing that could explain the apparition's presence.

With each cleared room, the tension in the "brain room" grew, a silent acknowledgment of the unknown we were confronting. The absence of a logical source for the apparition, the clear impossibility of the situation, settled around us like a shroud.

"What should we do?" Sierra asked me. "Should we go down and join them?"

"This place," I finally whispered, the words heavy with the weight of our discovery, "it's truly haunted." The realization was a turning point, a moment of clarity that shifted our investigation from a search for evidence to a confrontation with the unknown.

That's when we heard the elevator ding in the hallway. Macie smiled and breathed a sigh of relief. "They're on their way back."

But that wasn't right. I could see Midas opening bathroom stall doors and hear him and Cassidy chatting. Whomever was on the elevator wasn't Midas and Cassidy Demopolis.

Jericho and I exchanged a concerned glance but all four of us made our way to the open apartment door.

Just who in God's name was riding the elevator up?

Sierra reached for her radio as the elevator opened.

Chapter Seven—Macie

The air felt thicker as the elevator doors parted—a silent reveal to an empty void that chilled us to the core. An anticipatory silence had cocooned us as we waited, but the absence of anything in that small, confined space was more unnerving than any specter we had hoped or dreaded to find.

Cassidy and Midas emerged from the stairwell just behind us, a momentary reprieve that did little to dispel the growing unease among the team.

"Holy crap, guys! You scared me!" I shouted at them.

"We checked the entire floor. It's empty," Cassidy announced, her voice cutting through the tense atmosphere. The confirmation did little to ease the knot in my stomach. The idea of an empty elevator autonomously arriving to greet us was disconcerting, to say the least—a silent herald of the unknown forces we were attempting to uncover within the RSA Battle House Tower.

The moment served as a stark reminder of our vulnerability, a group of living, breathing beings seeking answers in a realm that defied the laws of nature and science as we understood them. The tower, with its storied past and spectral inhabitants, seemed to be watching, waiting to see what our next move would be.

In the midst of our collective trepidation, Midas stood resolute, a beacon of fearless curiosity. His eyes, alight with the thrill of the unknown, scanned the faces of his comrades, seeking an unspoken permission to delve deeper into the mystery that had just presented itself.

"I'll go down," I declared, my voice steady but charged with an unmistakable excitement. "I need to do this—by myself." My announcement was met with a chorus of protests, particularly from Jericho, whose concern for me was palpable in his tight expression and furrowed brow.

"No, it's too risky," he argued, his protective instinct clashing with my determined autonomy. But my mind was made up, my decision rooted in a confidence that bordered on recklessness—or perhaps, a deeper understanding of the task at hand.

Typical me. Go in, guns blazing, without thinking.

With a reassuring smile that did little to ease our worries, I stepped into the elevator, my solitary figure a stark contrast to the group I left behind. As the doors closed, sealing my fate, the rest of the team retreated to the brain room, our makeshift command center, to watch over me through the lens of the cameras we had painstakingly set up.

The second floor awaited me, silent and brooding, as if it held the key to the mysteries that wrapped the RSA Battle House Tower in whispers and shadows.

And I, Macie Graves, with my big mouth and unyielding spirit and sometimes unique talents, was stepping into the heart of it all, determined to uncover what lay hidden beneath the veil of darkness and fear.

The elevator's descent felt like a slow dive into another world, the soft hum of its mechanics a solitary comfort as the doors slid open to the second floor.

Stepping out, I found myself enveloped by an oppressive silence, the weight of unseen eyes almost tangible in the air. The darkness stretched out before me, punctuated only by the dim glow of emergency lights that cast long, sinister shadows across the empty hallway.

Finding a spot directly in view of one of our strategically placed cameras, I settled down with my notebook and pen, a familiar yet suddenly foreign ritual in these unnerving surroundings.

The camera's red recording light blinked steadily, a silent sentinel in the quiet, a reminder that, although physically alone, my team's gaze was fixed on me, a thread of connection in the enveloping gloom. It suddenly occurred to me that I did not bring a radio.

Well, did I need one? It's not like they couldn't see me.

In the shadowed silence of the second floor, my hands trembled as I opened my notebook, the chill of the unknown wrapping around me like a cold shroud.

Poised with my pen above the blank page, I was acutely aware of how charged the atmosphere was, teeming with whispers from the beyond that brushed against the edges of my consciousness. The profound sense of isolation was a stark, biting contrast to the distant warmth of my team, now just ethereal watchers through the camera's unblinking eye.

As my focus deepened, trying to forge a connection across the veils of reality, the oppressive silence of the hallway seemed to constrict around me.

Every soft shuffle, every breath-like whisper that drifted through the air, spiked my pulse and drew my eyes upward, searching the consuming darkness for a form, a shadow—anything. Yet, each time, only emptiness greeted me, a void where light dared not linger.

Okay, now I wish I had a radio.

Surrounded by the palpable loneliness of my solitary vigil, armed with nothing more than a pen and the fragile hope of contact, the weight of my vulnerability pressed down like a physical force. Driven by a blend of fear and resolve, I sought to reach out to the entity stirring in the tower's heart, to pierce the silence with a plea for understanding.

Then, as if guided by an unseen hand, my pen began to dance across the paper in a tempest of scribbles, lines tangling into forms too chaotic to discern. It moved with a will not my own, tracing the madness of spirits long silenced, their voices clamoring to be heard through the ink's wild gyre.

Yet, amidst the storm of motion, no words emerged, only the enigmatic ballet of a pen bewitched, leaving behind a cryptic mosaic that mocked my efforts to decipher it.

In that moment, surrounded by whispers of the past and the oppressive embrace of the tower, I was truly alone.

Each scratch of the pen, each phantom sound that caressed my ear, was a reminder of the vast gulf between our world and theirs—a gulf I was powerless to bridge with mere ink and paper.

Despite my concentration, despite my desperation to make contact, the page remained a mess of lines and curves, a frustrating testament to the elusive nature of whatever was with us in the tower. The sounds around me continued, a soft rustling, a whisper of movement that seemed always just out of sight, heightening the sense of dread that clung to the air.

It was a moment of profound isolation, a realization that, despite the technology and the team waiting above, I was truly alone here, with only the unseen for company.

The scribbles on the page mocked me, a chaotic reminder of the distance between our worlds, and of the immense challenge that lay in bridging that gap. The man in black, the sounds that teased the edges of my hearing, the oppressive silence—all of it converged in that moment, a haunting symphony of the unknown that I was powerless to decipher.

As I sat there, surrounded by darkness and unanswered questions, the tower seemed to close in around me, a maze of history and mystery that we had only just begun to explore.

The second floor, with its eerie silence and elusive shadows, was just the beginning, and I, Macie Graves, was right at the heart of it, a lone seeker in the vast, uncharted territory of the paranormal.

The shadows of the second floor seemed to stretch and contort as I gazed at the chaotic dance of scribbles sprawled across my notebook—a testament to my futile attempt to connect with the unseen. The frustration that bubbled within me was a heavy, suffocating cloak, made all the more unbearable by the isolation of my surroundings.

Holding the notebook up to the camera, I sought to share my failure with the team, the scrawls a silent scream of my vexation.

The scribbles, erratic and devoid of any discernible message, felt like a mocking echo of the silence that enveloped me. *What am I doing wrong?*

It wasn't long before Cassidy, armed with a radio and her ever-present determination, appeared beside me. I didn't even hear the elevator ding. I'd been so immersed in the process.

"Let me see," she insisted, her voice cutting through the heavy air like a beacon. As Cassidy's eyes scanned the page, a spark of recognition flickered across her face. "This...this looks like French script," she murmured, a note of excitement threading through her words. "It's old French, but definitely. Yeah, French."

The revelation was a jolt of electricity, igniting a flame of hope in the darkness of my frustration. *French? Why French?* But before I could drown in a sea of questions, Cassidy's radio crackled to life, Midas's voice tinged with curiosity and concern.

"French? You sure?" he asked, the skepticism in his voice unable to mask the intrigue that underpinned his words.

"Yes," Cassidy confirmed, her gaze locked on the notebook as if it held the key to the enigma of the RSA Battle House Tower. "Macie, keep going. You're making contact. Her name might be Helene. I think I can make that word out. Something about a baby. We'll have to use translating software but I think you're getting a real message. I mean, I went to art school in France, for a little while but I'm not that proficient."

That's when Sierra's voice, laden with a mix of astonishment and apprehension, broke through the static of the radio. "Helene... I saw her in my dream last night," she confessed, her words sending ripples through the still air. "I didn't tell you guys but yeah. I saw her. She was running through a swamp."

The revelation sent a shiver down my spine, a confluence of dream and reality that blurred the lines between the two. Sierra's dream, my scribbles, and Cassidy's insight wove together into a tapestry of mystery that seemed to envelop us all.

Encouraged by Cassidy's presence and the sudden breakthrough, I returned to my notebook with renewed vigor, the pen now a conduit between worlds, guided by forces unseen.

The possibility of making contact, of bridging the gulf that separated us from Helene, was a beacon in the darkness, a glimmer of understanding in the shadowed depths of the unknown.

As I scribbled, the whispers of the past seemed to grow louder, a chorus of voices reaching out from the void, eager to be heard.

The tower, with its secrets and its shadows, was speaking, and I, Macie Graves, was listening, determined to unravel the mystery that had drawn us into its heart.

Cassidy's fingers flew over the keyboard of her laptop, translating the scribbles that I had laid down on paper in a trance-like state. She'd brought her backpack with her, and I had no idea she'd brought her tablet too.

The hallway was silent, save for the soft tapping of keys and the occasional murmur of concentration from Cassidy. The anticipation was palpable as fragments of Helene's story began to emerge from the chaos of my automatic writing.

"It's... tragic," Cassidy finally spoke, her voice tinged with disbelief and sorrow.

I paused my scribbling as I began to process what I was experiencing. "Helene... She was accused of something, a crime. It's not clear, but it's tied to the land, right where the tower stands now. There's mention of a baby, a loss so profound it echoes through her words."

Reflecting on the connection we'd established with Helene, I felt an overwhelming mix of awe and responsibility. To think that our investigation had bridged centuries, connecting us to a spirit so desperate to be understood, to have her story told, was both humbling and daunting.

Spent and unable to continue. I called it. "Cassidy, I think I'm done." I couldn't help but cry and she let me cry on her shoulder like a big baby. If the man in black was around he didn't show himself. Soon, the team gathered around us, the mood somber as we discussed the implications of our findings. It was clear now that our investigation was much more than a simple ghost hunt; it had evolved into a quest for justice, a search for the truth behind the veil of time and death.

"Her story... it's part of the tower now," I mused aloud, the realization dawning on me. "Whatever happened to Helene, it's etched into the very walls, a piece of the tower's hidden secrets."

The discussion that followed was a whirlwind of theories and plans, a collective determination to uncover the full extent of Helene's tale. The connection we'd forged with her spirit was a beacon, guiding us deeper into the mysteries of the RSA Battle House Tower, compelling us to continue our exploration, to bring light to the shadows that lingered in the heart of the building.

As we wrapped up the session, the notebook filled with the echoes of Helene's voice, I couldn't shake the feeling that we were on the cusp of something profound.

Helene's story, whatever it might be, was intrinsically linked to the tower and its legacy, a puzzle piece in the vast, intricate history that we were only just beginning to piece together.

With each revelation, each whisper from the past, we were not only uncovering the secrets of the RSA Battle House Tower but also honoring the memory of those who had walked its halls, their stories waiting to be told, their truths waiting to be revealed.

And in the center of it all was Helene, a spirit caught between worlds, her tale a testament to the tower's haunted legacy.

We hung out a few more hours but nothing else happened. No strange appearances of Hyram or the Man in Black. Nothing at all. Around two in the morning, Midas called it.

We left the tower feeling emptied, sad but hopeful.

I had no idea the worst was to come.

72

Chapter Eight—Sierra

The sunlight filtering through the blinds of Gulf Coast Paranormal's office seemed out of place, too bright and cheerful for the mood that hung over us. It was the afternoon after our unsettling visit to the RSA Battle House Tower, and the team had gathered to discuss what we'd encountered.

I'd ordered pizzas, hoping to lighten the atmosphere, but even the familiar comfort food couldn't dispel the weight of our experiences. *Yeah, pepperoni can't fix everything. I sure do love it though.*

As everyone settled around the cluttered table, laden with pizza and paper plates, Macie broke the silence. "I've never channeled French cursive before," she confessed, her voice tinged with awe and a hint of trepidation. "I had the weirdest dreams last night. I'm not one to dream but wow. This poor person."

Her revelation the night before had added a new layer of complexity to our investigation, intertwining past and present in ways we were only beginning to understand. I nodded but didn't invite her to share. Not yet. We needed everyone here before we got started on this briefing.

Jericho was running late, a rarity for him. He'd texted earlier, mentioning he was stopping by his grandmother's church to pick up some supplies he felt we might need—holy water among them. His belief in the protective power of the items, sourced from a place of faith, offered a stark contrast to the technology and scientific methods we typically relied on. I couldn't fault him for that.

Big Brother had been hanging out in his office with the door shut. He was arguing with one of his cousins. Apparently, running the family fortune was quite stressful. Cassidy and I exchanged knowing glances and she shook her head with a frown.

Everyone else had arrived on time, carrying the weight of the night's events in their silence. Cassidy had brought baby Dominic along, a beacon of innocence and joy amidst our somber reflections. With his dark hair and eyes, he looked so much like his father. I could imagine that he would favor him very much, the older he got.

As we took turns cuddling the playful toddler, the tension in the room eased slightly, his giggles a reminder of the life that continued outside the shadows we chased. I snuck him some pizza and even gave him a sip of soda before his mom busted me.

I distributed slices of pizza in a vain attempt to lighten the mood, Cassidy juggled baby Dominic on her knee, casting me a look of mock sternness.

"Okay, Aunt Sierra, no more soda for Dom. He won't sleep tonight, and then you'll be on babysitting duty," she warned, her voice light but firm. Dominic, in his infinite baby wisdom, chose that moment to swipe at the baby wipe with a squeal of protest, smearing tomato sauce further across his cheek.

I chuckled, deflecting with a promise. "Deal. But you know I'd babysit him any day."

Midas slipped into the room then, a shadow of concern behind his eyes that he tried to mask with a brief smile for the team. We all noticed the undercurrent of his family's legacy, a silent presence among us.

"Everything okay, Midas?" I ventured, a careful balance of concern and respect for his privacy.

He nodded, settling into a chair with a heavy sigh. "Just family stuff. Let's focus on why we're here." Yet, his attempt to steer the conversation away couldn't erase the worry etched in his features.

Cassidy reached out, touching his arm in a silent show of support. "We're here for you, Midas. Always," she said softly, embodying the deep bond that tethered us all together.

As the meeting officially started, my focus shifted to leading our discussion. "Last night was intense," I began, eyeing each member of our assembled team. "We encountered more than we bargained for, especially with that figure in the tri corner hat and Macie's... French connection."

Laughter punctuated the tension, Macie's bemused shrug acknowledging the oddity of her newfound linguistic skills.

The doorbell jangled as Jericho, finally joined us, brandished a small vial of holy water with a flourish. "Brought some extra protection," he announced, placing it on the table among the pizza boxes. "Grandma insists it'll help."

Cassidy raised an eyebrow, a grin playing at her lips. "Well, if it's Grandma's idea, who are we to argue?"

The discussion that followed wove between analysis and speculation; our collective efforts aimed at unraveling the night's mysteries. Macie leaned forward, eager, and animated. "I never thought my scribbles would lead us here, talking about ghosts and history."

"And French cursive," Joshua added, his technical mind always looking for patterns, even in the paranormal.

As we mapped out our next steps, a sense of purpose solidified among us. The RSA Battle House Tower's history, layered with our personal experiences, demanded our attention, our respect.

"I say we bless ourselves with that holy water before heading out tonight," Cassidy suggested, her voice tinged with humor but underscored by a real acknowledgment of the unknown we were facing.

Nods of agreement circled the table, a moment of levity bridging our resolve and the daunting task ahead. The tower awaited us, its stories, its secrets, ensconced within walls that had seen centuries pass.

"We're in this together," Midas stated, a leader once more, the earlier shadows in his eyes replaced by determination. "Let's uncover the truth, for Helene, for all of us."

The buzz of conversation and the rustle of pizza boxes filled the room as I prepared to share what I'd uncovered. I grabbed another slice of pepperoni, using it to punctuate my points as I spoke. "So, I did some digging into the tower's history," I started, catching the team's attention. "Found out there were a bunch of accidents during its construction."

Midas, his mouth full of pizza, raised an eyebrow in interest. "Fatalities?" he mumbled, reaching for a napkin.

"None," I replied, shaking my head. "No deaths, which is unusual, right? Construction projects that big, you'd expect at least one or two, unfortunately. But nada."

Cassidy, gently bouncing Dominic on her lap, looked thoughtful. "That's weird, though. No deaths, but we're dealing with an apparition that seems... old. Like, really old."

"Yeah," I agreed, leaning back in my chair. "It doesn't add up. The man in the tri corner hat, his clothing—it's from a much earlier time. Our ghost—or whatever he is—doesn't seem to be a result of the construction."

Macie, scribbling something in her notebook, paused and looked up. "Maybe it's the land. Could it be something to do with what was here before the tower?"

"That's a possibility," I nodded, intrigued by the thought. "I checked into early Mobile history, but there's a lot to sift through. We might be looking at something—or someone—from a long, long time ago."

Joshua, fiddling with a piece of tech, chimed in. "This makes our job harder. How do we connect the dots if we're dealing with centuries of history?"

"We keep digging," Midas decided, his voice firm. "We've got to understand who this entity is and why it's here. Sierra, great job on the research. Let's all prepare to dive deeper tonight. We have no idea what we're up against."

The room fell into a thoughtful silence, the gravity of our situation settling in. As we finished our pizza, the camaraderie of the team was a tangible force, a shared determination to face whatever the tower held.

"Alright, let's see the creep again. Maybe we can get more clues," Midas suggested. I agreed with him.

Gathering around the large monitor, the afterglow of our team meeting faded into a focused intensity. I cued up the footage from the second floor, the image of the apparition clear against the backdrop of a dimly lit hallway. The figure, clad in a black suit and tri corner hat, stood out with an undeniable presence that demanded our attention once more.

"As you can see," I started, pointing to the screen where the figure loomed, "this wasn't just a trick of the light or a shadow playing tricks on us. He's too... defined, too real. And he doesn't appear to cast a shadow. This isn't a living person."

Joshua leaned in, his analytical mind searching for a logical explanation even in the face of the unexplainable. "It's like he was waiting for us, knowing we'd be watching," he mused, the hint of disbelief in his voice a testament to the apparition's clarity. "But why the second floor? All the activity happens on the fourth floor."

"Maybe he wanted to lure us off the fourth floor. I don't know." Cassidy, with Dominic now asleep in her arms, squinted at the screen. "He's not just a ghost from our time, trying to scare us. Look at him, he's from another era entirely."

The room fell into a contemplative silence, the implications of our observation settling heavily among us. The apparition, with his dated attire and knowing gaze, was a puzzle piece that didn't fit into the straightforward narrative of a haunted tower. He was a bridge to the past, a reminder that the stories we sought to uncover spanned far beyond the recent history we'd initially focused on.

"Whatever message he's trying to convey, it's rooted deep in the tower's history," Macie added, her voice tinged with awe and a dash of fear. "And he chose to reveal himself to us, to make sure we'd notice."

To be honest, I didn't get the sense that he had a message for us. Not at all. Except he wanted us to get out. He hated us. Hated everyone. Somehow, he hated Helene too. I swallowed as I thought about that and instinctively wiped a tear from my eye. Luckily, no one seemed to notice.

The realization was a sobering one, wrapping the investigation in layers of time and mystery that we were only beginning to unravel. The figure in the triangular hat was not just a ghost; he was a guardian of secrets, of stories long buried beneath the modern façade of the RSA Battle House Tower.

Turning from the screen, I opened my laptop, a collection of historical documents and notes arrayed before me. "There's something else," I began, the team's attention shifting to me. "His clothing, it's not just old, it's from a much earlier time than any recent deaths associated with the tower. Gianni and Sarah said the man was wearing a tri cornered hat. This has to be the guy, right? What are the odds? "

The team leaned in, the puzzle of the apparition deepening with every new piece of information. "This tower, its history... it's built on more than just the land we see today. There were lives here, stories that predate its construction," I continued, scrolling through digital archives of early Mobile's history.

Jericho, ever the skeptic, raised an eyebrow. "So, you're saying this ghost, our man in the triangular hat, is from what? The 1800s? Earlier?"

"Exactly," I affirmed, meeting his gaze. "His presence, his attire, suggests a connection to this place that goes back much further than the tower's construction. It hints at a history we've yet to uncover, stories woven into the very fabric of the land on which the tower now stands."

The room was silent, the weight of history pressing down upon us. The figure in the tri corner hat was not merely a haunting; he was a testament to a time long passed, a link to the deeper, older tales that the ground beneath the RSA Battle House Tower held.

"We're not just dealing with recent spirits or unexplained phenomena," I concluded, my voice steady but filled with an excited tremor. "We're touching on something much older, much more complex."

The team sat back, the scope of our investigation expanding before our eyes. The apparition on the second floor was more than a spectral presence; he was a guide, leading us into the depths of history, inviting us to uncover the stories that had been buried alongside the foundation of the tower itself.

As we contemplated our next move, the ghost in the tri corner hat lingered on the screen, a silent sentinel watching over our deliberations, his presence a bridge to the past that we were now tasked with crossing.

As the team settled into the revelations of the previous night, my focus shifted to the broader canvas of Mobile's history. "Consider this," I began, the room quieting down to listen, "the tower stands on what used to be swamp land."

Joshua, ever the pragmatist, interjected, "Well, not all of Mobile was swamp, Sierra. But yes, significant portions were." His clarification did little to dampen my enthusiasm.

"The significance isn't just geographical; it's historical, spiritual even. This Helene, she's ensnared in the swamp, not just figuratively but literally, according to what Cassidy's drawn and what I've seen." The pieces were starting to fit together, painting a picture that reached far beyond the recent history we'd initially focused on.

"The land remembers," I continued, my voice steady with conviction. "And whatever happened here, whatever stories were born from this swamp, they're key to understanding the haunting."

The insight shifted our focus, pulling us away from the surface level of recent events and deep into the layers of the past, urging us to consider not just the tower but the very ground it stood on. The weight of our discoveries hung in the air, a tangible presence that pushed us toward a decision. Midas, ever the leader, voiced his support. "Sierra's right. We need to go back, not just for Sarah and Cal, but to uncover the truth buried beneath the tower."

Cassidy laughed and it was a sweet sound. "Was there ever any doubt? Of course we're going back." She lifted chunky Dominic up on her shoulder and patted his back lovingly. About that time, their babysitter, Candy, knocked on the door before stepping into the office.

"Hey, Candy. He's sleeping well. He skipped his nap today so he might sleep awhile. If he's a bit jazzed later, blame Aunt Sierra. She gave him soda." Cassidy frowned at me playfully.

"He's an angel. Want to help me get him in the car?" Candy asked as she waved goodbye to us.

"Of course," Cassidy said as she reached for her son's bag. Midas swooped in and kissed his sleeping son's pizza sauce face.

Our resolve was tested in that moment, the enormity of our task dawning on us. Then, the phone rang, slicing through the tension with its shrill tone. I reached for it, answering with the speaker for all to hear. It was Sarah, her voice tinged with urgency and fear.

"Midas, hold on. It's Sarah," I stopped him from leaving with Cassidy and Candy. "I'm putting you on speakerphone, if that's okay. The whole team is here."

"Sure, no problem. Something's happened on the fourth floor," she said, her words quick and breathless. "You need to come back. Now. It's destroyed. The apartment, all your gear. It's destroyed."

Joshua rose from his chair. "All the equipment?"

The room fell silent, the gravity of her words settling over us. This wasn't just another investigation; it was a call to action, a plea for help from beyond the veil that separated our world from the next.

"We'll be there, Sarah," Midas promised, his voice firm, the decision made. The team nodded in agreement, a silent pact forming among us. "Give us an hour, okay. Don't touch anything. Don't worry about cleaning anything up. We need to photograph everything first and then we'll tidy up the mess."

"If you say so," she said before hanging up the phone.

As she ended the call, the urgency of Sarah's voice echoed in our minds, a reminder of the unknown we were about to face. The decision to return was made with a mix of fear and determination, a recognition that we were stepping into a mystery far greater than any we had encountered before.

The meeting concluded, but the energy in the room had shifted. We were united, our purpose clear. We would return to the tower, to the heart of the haunting, armed with our newfound knowledge and an unwavering resolve to face whatever awaited us in the shadows.

The history of Mobile, the mystery of poor, pregnant Helene, and the haunting of the tower were intertwined, each a thread in a tapestry we were only beginning to unravel.

As we prepared to leave, the sense of purpose was palpable, each of us ready to confront the past and its hold on the present.

The tower awaited, its secrets cloaked in shadow, but we were no longer just investigators.

We were seekers of truth, determined to shine a light into the darkness and reveal the stories that had been silenced for too long.

Chapter Nine–Midas

The van was packed to the brim, the hum of anticipation palpable as I called the team together for a final briefing before we embarked on our second night at the RSA Battle House Tower. The air was thick with tension, a tangible manifestation of our collective unease and determination.

Each of us knew the stakes had risen, the shadows we pursued now seemed to reach back towards us with an intent we could only guess at.

"Laser grids, REM pods, K2 meters," I began, ticking off the list of our arsenal against the unseen, "check them twice. We can't afford any equipment failures tonight." Heads nodded in agreement, the flicker of LED lights from the gear casting an otherworldly glow on determined faces.

Joshua, who had been unusually quiet, shifted uncomfortably. "I'm bringing the RYDER," he finally admitted, his voice a mix of resolve and apprehension. The admission hung in the air, a weighty decision given the device's controversial history within our team.

I met his gaze, understanding the gravity of his choice. "Good," I responded, the single word an acknowledgment of the seriousness with which we approached the night's endeavor. "We need every advantage we can get."

The mood as we loaded up was somber yet focused, each of us mentally preparing for what lay ahead. The darkness of the tower loomed in our minds, a silent challenge that whispered threats and promises in equal measure.

"Stay in pairs," I reminded them, the command more a plea for their safety than anything else. "We don't know what we're dealing with, and I won't have anyone taking unnecessary risks."

As we double-checked our equipment, the reality of our investigation pressed in on us. The laser grids, capable of revealing the slightest disturbances in their beams; the REM pods, sensitive to the movements of energies unseen; the K2 meters, flickering in response to the presence of the paranormal—all were tools in our quest to pierce the veil of mystery that shrouded the tower.

The drive to the site was silent, each of us lost in our thoughts, the weight of our previous encounter a shadow that stretched long into the night. How much damage had been done to our equipment? Was it a human culprit or an otherworldly attacker? I prayed we had video to help us determine the answer.

The cold embrace of the RSA Battle House Tower welcomed us back into its shadowed halls, the silence a stark contrast to the cacophony of our thoughts as we ascended to the fourth floor. The atmosphere was charged, each step heavier than the last, our breaths shallow in anticipation of the destruction we feared awaited us.

At least the lights were on and of course, Midas wasn't having that. He and Cal went to the breaker room and flicked the lights off for the bottom four floors.

Cal and Sarah, their expressions a mixture of apology and concern, met us at the entrance to our makeshift command center. "We're sorry about the mess. I can't explain it," Sarah whispered, her eyes darting away, unable to meet ours directly. They quickly excused themselves, leaving us to the eerie quiet of the tower, a silent witness to the night's forthcoming trials.

The door creaked open, revealing a scene of chaos that was somehow less devastating than we had braced for.

Monitors were askew, one tragically cracked beyond repair, a casualty of the unseen forces we were here to confront. The cameras, our silent sentinels, had been displaced, their angles altered as if to blind us to something we were not meant to see.

Without a word, we each set to work, each of us driven by a need to restore order, to reclaim our foothold in this place that seemed so determined to reject our presence.

As we righted cameras and recalibrated equipment, the REM pods sprang to life, their lights flashing urgently, a beacon of the presence that lingered just beyond our sight. Macie and I exchanged surprised glances, she was helping me right the largest of the monitors.

"Trippy. We've got company," she said as she waited for the REM pod to calm down. "I think we should get started, y'all. Don't you?"

The air grew colder, a palpable shift in the atmosphere that heralded the start of our EVP (Electronic Voice Phenomenon) session.

The digital recorder, placed at the center of the room, became our conduit to the other side, a bridge across the chasm that separated our worlds.

And then, the voices began, a symphony of whispers that curled around us like smoke.

"Leave...danger...not welcome..." The words, fragmented and chilling, wove into the fabric of the night, a tapestry of warning that we could not ignore.

Our equipment, the laser grids casting nets of green light, the K2 meters flickering in response, became our eyes and ears in the darkness. The tower, with its secrets and its shadows, seemed to come alive around us, a presence both ancient and angry, reaching out from the depths of history to touch the living.

The messages, captured in the static of the recorder, were a puzzle, each piece a fragment of a story that we were only beginning to uncover. The words immediately began flowing from the machine.

Emma. Where are you?

What?

Get out!

Three, two, one...

Sierra, please. Watch your step.

Each voice seemed different but the one calling for Sierra was female, or so it sounded. The weight of command settled heavily on me as we ventured into the shadow-laced depths of the second floor.

The green glow from our laser grid painted an eerie tapestry across the hall, casting long shadows that seemed almost alive, twisting and coiling with a life of their own. It was a hunter's setup, designed to reveal what usually remained unseen, yet the beauty of the technology offered little solace against the creeping dread that this place instilled. Frankly, the laser grid was one of my favorite tools. It was easy to catch shadow play against a grid.

I glanced at Joshua, noting the RYDER clutched in his hands, his anticipation palpable. "This could be the perfect time to test it," he suggested, barely containing his eagerness to unleash the device's potential.

I hesitated, the weight of responsibility pressing down. The RYDER was powerful, unpredictable, and in a place as charged as the RSA Battle House Tower, who knew what it might provoke? "Wait," I cautioned, the decision heavy on my tongue. "We don't know what we're dealing with yet. We will use it tonight, just not yet."

Our standoff was brief but charged, a silent struggle between curiosity and caution in the face of the unknown.

Joshua was like a little brother to me, extremely stubborn and always ready to try something new. Yeah, we were a lot alike.

We stood there in the dim light, watching, waiting, when suddenly, a shadow flickered across the grid. It was swift, too swift, a formless thing that seemed to defy the laws of physics as it scuttled across the ceiling.

"There!" I pointed, my voice a harsh whisper in the stillness. The shadow twisted and turned, an impossible movement that seemed to mock our attempts to understand it. "You see it, right?" I pointed my handheld camera in that direction in case the static camera missed the movement.

"Hell yeah, I see it!" Joshua's fingers tightened around the RYDER, a silent echo of his frustration. He was ready, eager even, to confront whatever haunted this place, but the risk of escalation was too great.

With a curt nod, he acknowledged that he had indeed seen it, though I could see the impatience simmering beneath his calm exterior.

To my shock and horror, the shadow climbed up the wall, hung from the ceiling, on all fours and then vanished.

"It's moved to the third floor," I announced, the realization dawning that this game of cat and mouse spanned far beyond the simple corridors and rooms we navigated. This entity, whatever it was, played by rules we barely understood, slipping through the very fabric of the building with ease. I pretended that my knees didn't pop as I got up off the floor.

"I better radio the rest of the team," I said aloud, my mind racing with the implications of our encounter. The tower, with all its secrets and shadows, was more than just a structure; it was a nexus of energies, ancient and modern, that we were only just beginning to unravel.

"Guys. I don't know if you saw that, but it is headed your way."

"Roger that, Midas. We're ready," Sierra's voice sounded confident. "Jericho is coming down."

As we prepared to follow the shadow's path, the reality of our investigation into the unknown weighed heavily on me. We were charters of the unseen, seekers of truths hidden in the darkness, and tonight, the tower seemed all too eager to share its secrets.

The tension on the third floor was palpable, a thick cloak of anticipation and fear that settled over us as we moved through the dimly lit hallways.

Jericho, ever the even-keeled investigator, manned one of the handheld cameras, sweeping its lens across the dark corners and long stretches of corridor that characterized the RSA Battle House Tower's haunting architecture.

It was during one of these routine sweeps that Jericho froze, his breath catching in a sharp intake. "Holy hell. Did you see that?" he hissed, voice barely above a whisper, the camera's night vision casting an eerie green glow on his face.

We crowded around him, peering into the small screen of the camera, where, for a moment, a face seemed to materialize outside the window—a floor too high for any mundane explanation. The face was a blur of features, indistinct yet unmistakably human, pressed against the glass as if seeking entry or perhaps trying to communicate a silent plea.

The footage, once reviewed, left us more baffled than reassured. The sighting was clear, yet its impossibility twisted our understanding into knots. How could a face appear at a window several stories high, with no ledge or foothold in sight?

Jericho, doubting his own eyes, shook his head in disbelief. "No way I imagined it," he muttered, but the uncertainty in his voice betrayed his internal struggle. Macie, ever the empath, placed a comforting hand on his shoulder.

"Hey, where's that holy water? Why not apply some to the windows? At least to the windows we can get to. The apartments are all locked, but we can anoint the rest of the windows."

Her suggestion hung in the air, a potential course of action against the unease that had settled upon us. Yet, I hesitated, aware of the delicate balance we tread in this investigation.

"We don't want to tick it off," I finally said, my voice firm yet cautious. The realm we were interacting with, filled with shadows and whispers, was not one to be provoked lightly. "I like the idea, let's collect more evidence first though."

The idea of using holy water, a symbol of purity and protection, was appealing yet fraught with uncertainty. The entity or entities we were dealing with operated on rules and logic far removed from our own. To assume our actions would be understood, let alone respected, was a gamble. I cared about my team and the last thing I wanted to do was put them in further danger.

The night stretched on, a tapestry of shadows and light, as we continued our investigation, each moment a brushstroke in a picture that was slowly coming into focus. The face at the window remained an enigma, a silent sentinel that watched over us as we delved deeper into the mysteries of the RSA Battle House Tower.

That's when Sierra decided to shake things up. And I could tell by the look on her face that there was no arguing with her.

"I have to do a walkthrough, Midas. I'm not getting anything here, except residual energy and poor Hyram. I want to walk the property. Walk around the building."

"I'll go with her," Cassidy offered as she reached for the handheld camera and checked the battery to see how much power she had left. I glanced at Joshua who was raising an eyebrow at his wife while still holding RYDER.

"Fine. Cassidy, Sierra, you go for the walk. Macie, man the monitors."

"Sorry, boss, but I'm going with the other ladies. Girl power and all that."

I nodded in agreement, not it mattered apparently.

I prayed to God I wasn't making a huge mistake.

Chapter Ten-Sierra

As we gathered our gear in the dimly lit room, the air was thick with anticipation and an unspoken anxiety that seemed to press down on my shoulders like a heavy cloak. I didn't need any equipment, but I was willing to wait for the other two psychics.

Cassidy, always the artist, clutched her worn khaki backpack, which held her sketchpad and pencils, her eyes alight with the thrill of capturing the unknown. She had insisted on accompanying me, eager to document any visions or spirits we might encounter through her art. Cassidy's presence was both a comfort and a reminder of the serious nature of our journey into the unknown.

Macie, with a determination that was both fierce and protective, declared she would handle the camera. It was her way of taking part, of ensuring that every moment was recorded, every shadow and whisper captured. Her resolve was palpable, a steady anchor in the swirling currents of our unease.

Midas, ever the cautious one, voiced his concerns with a furrowed brow. He didn't like the idea of us splitting up; the risks, he argued, were great, and the safety of the team should be our paramount concern. His words hung heavy in the air, a reminder of what was at stake.

Yet, the decision had been made, and the path set. His unease mirrored my own, a silent echo in the depths of my thoughts.

Joshua, with a tenderness that belied his rugged exterior, made sure his wife had a working radio. His concern was a tangible thing, a thread of worry that weaved through his actions.

Macie, taking the radio, declared she would be the one to hold onto it. Her decision was more than just practicality; it was a statement of her willingness to shoulder the burden, to ensure that I could walk without interruptions, my focus undivided as we stepped into the shadows.

For that, I was grateful.

As we stepped outside, the chill of the air seemed to grow colder, the shadows deeper, as we moved, guided by a pull that seemed to tug at the very core of my being. What lay ahead was unknown, a journey into the darkness that awaited us with open arms.

This is weird. It wasn't cold earlier.

Outside, the night wrapped around us with an intensity that seemed to muffle the very beats of our hearts, its darkness so complete it swallowed the feeble beams of our flashlights whole.

The air, heavy with the scent of damp earth and the ghostly perfume of day's end, seemed to murmur with secrets, its whispers carried on a wind that felt like the breath of the unseen.

Amidst the oppressive darkness, the grounds betrayed an eerie beauty, a stark contrast to the creeping dread that filled the air. The gardens, meticulously cared for, held an otherworldly charm under the moon's pale light.

Gardenias bloomed like specters in the night, their fragrance almost overwhelming, as if trying to mask a smell of something far less pleasant lurking beneath. Their white flowers practically glowed in the dark.

As we delved deeper, leaving the last comforting pools of light behind, the chill intensified, biting into our flesh with the promise of unseen horrors. It was a physical manifestation of the boundary between our world and the spectral, a boundary that felt all too thin at that moment.

At least it was for me. I wondered if Macie and Cassidy felt the same way. I didn't ask.

In this realm of shadow and uncertainty, I sensed the first stirrings of connection.

It was more than just a feeling—it was a force, pulling me towards something invisible, a presence that whispered directly to my soul.

This whisper wasn't comforting; it was a siren call from the abyss, beckoning with the promise of forbidden knowledge and hidden truths.

Oh yes, this was all too familiar to me.

The deeper we ventured into the gardens, the more the darkness seemed to press against us, a physical weight that sought to crush the very air from our lungs.

The gardenias, once a pleasant distraction, now seemed to mock us with their beauty, thriving in a place that felt increasingly malevolent.

It was here, in the embrace of a night that seemed alive with ancient, watchful things, that I realized our journey was not just a mere exploration but a descent into a realm that defied understanding.

The ground beneath our feet, so carefully tended, hid secrets far older and more terrifying than any ghost story. A body. Another body. Ugh. I could hear them sighing as they rested.

Deep under the ground but oh yes, there were bodies here. And it was these secrets that called to me, a whisper in the dark that I could not ignore, drawing me deeper into the night's embrace.

Helene? I hope you're not beneath my feet. I pray to God you escaped the mob that wanted to kill you.

Cassidy found a spot nearby, her eyes scanning the darkness for a glimpse of the unseen. With each step I took, with each breath of the chilled air, she began to sketch, her movements becoming increasingly frenetic as she tried to capture the essence of what I was encountering. Her pencils danced across the paper, a silent testament to the unseen forces that swirled around us.

"I'm right here, Sierra. Take your time."

Macie, her camera held steady, moved with a purpose, her gaze flickering between the viewfinder and the shadows that danced just beyond our reach. The soft click of the shutter was a steady heartbeat in the night, capturing moments of unseen terror and awe.

"Thank you," I whispered to her as I paused and waited to see what I would experience next. It was then, in the heart of the darkness, that I connected with the spirit of pitiful Helene.

Her presence was a whisper at first, a gentle touch against my consciousness that grew stronger with each passing moment. She'd been a lady once, a true Lady. Lady Helene Wayfarer of Essex County. Not here. There were no aristocrats in Mobile in those days, or this one either.

The air around me seemed to shimmer with our combined energy—Helene and mine, a soft glow illuminated the path ahead. Helene spoke French but somehow, I understood every word.

Helene's story wove its way into my consciousness as the night around us seemed to grow denser, charged with the echoes of a past long buried yet palpably alive within the whispering wind.

Helene's life was a haunting symphony of sorrow, a narrative that transcended time and death itself. She had made a horrible mistake—coming to America. I could hear her mother crying, begging her to stay in England. I could even hear the argument between them. "Helene, you will have nothing. No one. Only Mr. Dagurette. If he loves you, he will not drag you to the wilderness."

"Mother, dear. He's not dragging me anywhere. This is an adventure. You know how much I love an adventure!"

Helene lived in an era where faith dictated more than just the salvation of the soul; it commanded one's place in the community, their safety, their very existence.

She was a beacon of Protestant conviction in a village where such beliefs were more than just frowned upon—they were deemed anathema. The Catholic townsfolk, spurred by a zeal that bordered on fanaticism, saw Helene not as a neighbor but as a heretic, a stain upon the purity of their faith. She'd been teaching her servants her beliefs, but surely that wasn't a sin.

One fateful night, a mob formed, a roiling mass of anger and self-righteous fury that surged towards Helene's door with the inevitability of a storm. They demanded Helene's conversion, a renunciation of her beliefs in exchange for peace and acceptance within the community.

But Helene, with a strength that belied her gentle nature, refused. Her faith was her fortress, and she would not betray it, not even in the face of overwhelming hatred.

Her husband, whom she had believed to be her partner in both spirit and faith, stood silent. "Francis? Say something!"

Whether it was fear that stilled his tongue or a hidden concord with the mob's fervor, he did nothing, said nothing. At least before he'd had me run, run for my life, but how could I do that? The baby was too big in my belly and the swamp was dangerous. What was I to do?

In that moment of betrayal, Helene stood alone, a solitary figure of defiance against the darkness that sought to engulf her.

The mob's wrath was swift and merciless. The priest, Father Jerome Bastogne led the horrible group that demanded her conversion.

Helene's refusal to abandon her faith was met with violence, a brutality that was as senseless as it was savage. As they dragged her from her home, her cries for understanding, for mercy, were drowned out by the clamor of her accusers. They were the last sounds she uttered before the night swallowed her whole. She was literally dragged, her shoes came off, her feet were wet with blood as they were cut by the rocks.

Angry arms tugged at her, pinching and pulling at her skin.

And then, as quickly as the vision had come, it receded, leaving a lingering heaviness in the air.

The darkness that clung to the land seemed imbued with Helene's presence, a shroud of sorrow that blanketed everything it touched. Her voice, though faint, carried the weight of centuries, a plea not just for understanding, but for release from the eternal torment of being bound to a world that had shown her no mercy.

But why was she here? What did she want? I had no idea. Not yet.

In that moment, it became clear that Helene's tale was a reminder of the power of belief and the cost of standing firm in one's convictions in the face of overwhelming adversity.

And as her voice faded into the past and I stepped back into the present, a solemn vow formed in my heart—to help Helene find the release she so desperately sought, to untangle the threads of her story from the darkness that held her captive.

As I tearfully tried to relay Helene's story, Cassidy's sketching grew more desperate, her hands moving with a fervor that belied the chill in the air. Macie was staring at me like I had two heads.

I wonder what that's about?

I turned my attention to Cassidy's work. The images that took shape on her paper were a mirror to the tales of sorrow and longing that Helene shared, a visual echo of the spirit's plea. She nailed the scene, Helene's screaming face, the mob dragging her away, her husband Francis, watching without helping her.

The encounters that night were chilling, not just for the cold that seeped into our bones, but for the profound sense of connection that bridged the gap between our world and the next.

Macie, typically a beacon of resilience and strength, was unusually silent, her form shrouded in the dim light of our flashlights.

Sensing a shift in her demeanor, I ventured to ask if she was alright. The response was not what I expected. A single tear, glimmering like a jewel against the backdrop of the dark, traced a path down her cheek.

"You disappeared, Sierra," she whispered, her voice barely audible over the rustling of the leaves. "Right in front of me. You were here and then... you weren't here."

Her words sent a shiver down my spine, not from the chill of the night but from the raw fear they carried. I could only imagine what it must have been like for her, watching me vanish into thin air.

Without hesitation, I stepped forward and enveloped her in a hug, offering assurances that I was indeed okay and apologizing for the fright I had unwittingly caused.

As we stood there, wrapped in a moment of shared vulnerability, an eerie laughter sliced through the night, pulling us back to the grim reality of our surroundings.

"Oh no. Did you hear that?" Cassidy looked up from her sketching. "Disembodied voice."

Apparently they couldn't see him but I could. The source of the unsettling, diabolical laughter was a man donned in a tri-cornered hat, his figure barely discernible in the gloom.

He had not been a part of the mob that had sought to condemn Helene; his demeanor and attire set him apart from that time period. The mob had been a manifestation of zealous fury, led by a Catholic priest, but this man in the triangular hat was no priest.

He was something else altogether. His laughter carried a sinister edge, mocking our efforts, reveling in the fear that clung to the air.

Pray, darling Sierra. Pray for God's help.

And that quickly, I was Helene again. But it was at this moment, as the priest's intentions became clear—he was about to capture Helene—that Cassidy's urgent voice pulled me from the trance. The abruptness of the return to reality was disorienting, a stark contrast to the vividness of the vision that had consumed me.

"Hey, come back to us, Sierra. That's enough. You're as white as the moon."

Then, cutting through the tension, a static-laden call for help crackled through the radio, instantly drawing our attention. It was Jericho!

The urgency in his voice was unmistakable, a clarion call that snapped us into action. Whatever had prompted his distress was serious, and every instinct I possessed screamed that we needed to respond, and quickly.

The encounter with the man in the tri-cornered hat, his mocking laughter still echoing in our ears, was a chilling reminder of the complexities of the spiritual realm we were navigating.

But now, with Jericho's call pulling us back, our focus shifted. We were a team, and one of our own was in need.

The mysteries of the night and the echoes of the past would have to wait.

Chapter Eleven—Jericho

The moment the elevator shuddered to a halt between floors, a cold dread wrapped its fingers around my heart. The lights flickered sporadically, casting ghostly shadows against the walls, and then darkness engulfed me completely. The silence that followed was suffocating, pierced only by the erratic pounding of my own heart.

I reached out, my hands finding only the cold metal of the elevator walls—a tomb of steel and wires. My breaths came quick and shallow, the air stale and heavy, as if it too were afraid to move.

I called out, hoping for a response, but my voice seemed to be swallowed by the darkness itself. Trapped and alone, the reality of my situation settled in—a prey tethered in the dark, waiting.

Stay calm, dude. It's just a glitch. Just a glitch. That's all.

As I struggled against the rising panic, the elevator's lights began to flicker again with a frenetic energy, as if a storm were raging inside its circuits. Then, without warning, the elevator began moving. Quickly and upward.

The doors slid open and as I immediately stepped off the elevator, the air was thick with the scent of decay, and the silence was broken by distant, echoing footsteps.

What floor am I on?

Strangely enough, there was an odd fog on this floor. I still had no idea what floor I'd ended up on. My hand went to my walkie-talkie again. "Hey! I'm off the elevator but I don't know what floor I'm on and there's some sort of smoke."

Nobody answered me. I tapped the button again. Was the dang thing not working?

Amidst the fog, a figure emerged—a man cloaked in black, his eyes hollow pits of malice. He was the source, the heart of the tower's torment, roaming its halls with a presence so malevolent it seemed to warp the very fabric of reality. He was the reason for what was happening here on this land and in this tower. If he had the strength, he would affect the entire building, but he wasn't that strong. Not yet.

The boundary between past and present blurred, and I found myself caught in the eye of a storm that had raged for centuries. This man, in the tri-cornered hat, wearing a dirty black suit, stared at me hard.

I could hear the derogatory names he called me, not with my ears, but in my head. Strangely enough, his insults did not frighten me. They angered me.

Call me what you want. You don't belong here.

I belong where I am welcome. I am welcome here. You are not.

He walked toward me. One step, two step.

The air between us charged with an unseen energy, the man in the black suit took another step forward, his intent clear in the darkness of his gaze. I could feel the malevolence rolling off him in waves, a tangible force pressing against my spirit.

"What is your name?"

The strange entity did not answer me but laughed at my question. But rather than succumbing to fear, something within me ignited—a fire fueled by faith and a steadfast refusal to be intimidated by this harbinger of darkness.

"In the name of Jesus, I command you to leave!"

The words tore from my throat, not as a plea, but as a decree, echoing powerfully in the fog-shrouded corridor. The man halted, his sneer giving way to a momentary flicker of surprise. He responded, not aloud, but directly into my mind, with words laced in French, revealing snippets of his pursuit and desires.

It was a glimpse into the depth of his vendetta, a vendetta tied intricately not only to the tower, but colonial Mobile's sordid past. And then, with a disdainful laugh that seemed to resonate in the very walls, he dissipated like smoke on the wind, leaving behind a heavy silence and a lingering chill.

Just like that, all the fog sucked up into the ceiling, taking the unwanted monster with it. The elevator dinged behind me.

Shaken, but with a renewed sense of purpose, I approached the door, which was now curiously inviting rather than foreboding. The cabin was starkly illuminated, a beacon in the midst of lingering shadows.

Stepping inside, I pressed the button for the ground floor, half-expecting another plunge into darkness. But the elevator obeyed, descending smoothly, a gentle hum replacing the ominous silence of before. As the doors opened to reveal the familiar, albeit now comforting, confines of the lobby, a wave of relief washed over me.

The air was clear, free of the oppressive weight that had marked my journey thus far.

Climbing back into the elevator and descending to the bottom floor symbolized more than just a physical return; it was a reaffirmation of my resolve to confront whatever darkness lurked within the tower, armed with faith and a newfound understanding of the enemy.

The lobby, once a mere transition space, now felt like a haven as I stepped out of the elevator. Macie was the first to greet me, her expression a mix of concern and curiosity. Her thin arms went around me and I kissed her to let her know I was okay.

The rest of the team clustered around, their faces lit by the soft glow of the lobby lights, eager for an update.

As I recounted the harrowing encounter with the entity in the black suit, I could see the gravity of my experience reflected in their eyes. When I mentioned the entity's search for someone, Sierra interjected with a clarity that cut through the lingering tension, "Helene! That's who they were chasing!"

The pieces of the puzzle began to align, drawing us into a tighter circle of shared purpose. I both agreed with and disagreed with her thoughts about the entity searching for Helene.

My voice, steadier than I felt, carried the weight of my next words, "This is no mere ghost bent on revenge. It's something else."

Midas, usually unflappable, appeared visibly shaken. "A maelstrom?" he ventured. I shook my head and felt my girlfriend Macie sigh with relief beside me, the memory of the entity's malevolence fresh in my mind.

"No. But just as bad." The air between us was thick with the unspoken realization that we were dealing with a force beyond our current understanding. This is literally, the spirit of Religion." Nobody spoke for a minute, just stared at me like I was crazy. Maybe I was but I knew this without a shadow of a doubt.

We found a quiet corner of the lobby, a makeshift circle formed as we each took a turn to share what we had encountered. Sierra and Cassidy went first, their narrative a chilling account of their time outside.

Sierra spoke of the palpable sense of history and sorrow that pervaded the air, her words painting a picture as vivid as the reality she had walked through.

Cassidy, with a quiet intensity, unfolded her sketches across our makeshift table. Each stroke of her pencil brought the night's encounters to life—shadowy figures, twisted expressions of fear and longing, and, at the center of it all, Helene's tormented spirit.

The sketches were a visual echo of Sierra's words, a tangible link to the ethereal experiences they had faced. As we leaned in, the shared weight of our findings bound us together, a team united in the pursuit of understanding the darkness that haunted the tower.

"You guys have to see this," Macie announced, her voice cutting through the hushed tones of our discussions. She pulled out her camera, rewinding the footage to the crucial moment captured during our investigation.

As the footage played, a collective gasp echoed in the corner of the lobby we had claimed as our own. On the screen, Sierra, enveloped in a thick, almost sentient fog, stepped forward and then... vanished.

"That's what I saw upstairs. It moves in the mist, the fog!" I added as I studied the film.

It was as if the mist swallowed Sierra whole, leaving no trace behind. The clarity and suddenness of her disappearance were unsettling, to say the least.

"If I hadn't seen it with my own eyes, I wouldn't have believed it," I admitted, voicing the disbelief that hung heavily in the air. This footage, irrefutable and shocking, added a chilling layer of evidence to our investigation, grounding the ethereal experiences of the night in a stark reality that was impossible to ignore.

With the eerie silence of the lobby enveloping us, we turned our attention to the EVP recordings and laser grid footage collected by the indoor team. The static-filled whispers and unexplained shadows captured on tape suggested we were not alone in our experiences.

As the recordings played, the disembodied voices seemed to echo around us, a testament to the unseen presence that lingered in the tower. It was an array of voices and none that appeared pertinent to the investigation. Still, we listened, and I made sure that I'd replay it through our software just to be sure we weren't missing compelling evidence.

The laser grid footage was even more intriguing, with unexplained movements breaking the pattern of lights—shapes and figures that seemed to move with purpose, undetectable to the naked eye.

The evidence laid bare before us suggested we were dealing with a presence both powerful and ancient, a spirit or entity rooted deeply in the history of the tower.

This realization cemented our resolve to delve deeper into the mystery, to uncover the origins of the haunting and the desires of the spirits we had encountered.

Sierra tilted her head thoughtfully. "I think I'd like to try something, Big Brother. Don't freak out. Let the three of us work together. You know, like a mediums' roundtable." Midas frowned at that idea.

"I don't think it's a good idea," he murmured, skepticism plain in his voice. "Can't you do the same thing at the office?"

Yet, sensing the potential for groundbreaking insights, I, alongside Joshua, voiced our support for the endeavor. "We need to understand what we're dealing with, and this might be our best shot," I argued, my conviction bolstering the team's resolve. "It'll make a strong connection, Midas."

I could see that my friend wasn't completely on board, but he relented to what the team wanted to try.

Macie took the lead. It would be through automatic writing, they sought to bridge the gap between our world and the spirits', her hand moved across pages with a life of their own.

This collaborative psychic effort did not unveil the layers of the tower's haunted history. It did not reveal sorrowful tales or ancient grievances that had long been buried. It was more scribbling, presumably French that none of us understood. It was a somber experience that brought us closer together even if it didn't reveal any answers.

After about an hour, Midas called the second night's investigation, and we loaded up a ton of equipment. We planned to come back once more. Joshua was going to use RYDER tomorrow night, but in the meantime, I was going to prayer, to my grandmother's prayer group.

We needed spiritual discernment. Quick, fast and in a hurry.

The drive back to Gulf Coast Paranormal's headquarters was a mixture of silence and sporadic conversation, each of us lost in thought over the night's eerie revelations.

As we unloaded the equipment, the weight of new sketches, recordings, and personal accounts seemed to echo the heaviness in our hearts. The headquarters, usually a place of lively discussion and laughter, took on a somber air as we gathered to review our findings.

The sketches laid out across tables, the recordings ready to be analyzed, and the personal accounts waiting to be shared—all painted a picture of a haunting far more complex and deep-rooted than we had initially imagined.

Our return to the familiar surroundings of our offices marked not an end, but a beginning—a new chapter in our quest to understand the secrets hidden within the tower's walls.

We set about planning our next steps, our collective experiences from the night fueling our resolve to delve even deeper into the mystery that had enveloped us.

Finally, with tired eyes and a steady resolve, we left and went home. I dropped off Macie, resisting her invitation to stay over and headed to Grandma Rose's house.

Tomorrow was going to bring us the answers we needed. I was sure of it.

I hadn't planned on seeing the Man in Black standing on my grandmother's porch. Only for the briefest of seconds, but then he was gone.

I went inside, anointed the room with holy water, and passed out.

Chapter Twelve—Cassidy

As night cloaked the RSA Tower in shadows, we returned, our steps echoing in the silent anticipation of the unknown. The building loomed before us, a monolith of dark windows and whispered secrets. The air was palpable and thick, charged with a tension that seemed to seep from the very walls, a residue of our last visit's unearthly encounters.

I couldn't help but sigh deeply. As much as I wanted to help Sarah and the others, even Helene, I didn't want to be here. Not at all.

As we pulled up, I was surprised to see Cal met us at the entrance, his usual composure frayed at the edges. In the dim light, his face was etched with lines of worry, and his eyes darted about as if expecting the shadows to move.

"I...I found something after you all left," he began, his voice a notch above a whisper. "Footprints. Muddy, clear footprints on every floor. But no one's been in here, not since you guys..." His voice trailed off, lost amidst the creaking silence of the building. "Tell me you did that. I won't be mad about it. It's just, this is bad. The mud is everywhere. Not just the floors."

Midas glanced at me but neither of us said anything. What was there to say? We sure didn't muddy up the place.

He looked at us then, a silent plea in his gaze. "The residents... they're coming back tomorrow." The urgency in his voice was unmistakable, a stark reminder of the ticking clock hanging over our investigation. "I don't know if we should continue," he admitted, the words heavy with the weight of his fears. "Maybe this is enough."

His words sent a shiver down my spine, not just from the thought of unseen feet wandering these abandoned halls, but from the realization of what it meant.

Midas, always the pillar among us, met Cal's wavering resolve with a steadfast determination. "We're close, Cal. Closer than we've ever been," he said, his voice cutting through the thick air with a resolve that seemed almost out of place in the eerie quiet of the RSA Tower. "Give us tonight. By morning, we'll have answers." There was something in his tone, a kind of unshakeable confidence, that seemed to momentarily lift the weight of dread that hung over us.

I side eyed my husband. It wasn't like him to make those kinds of promises, but I could tell by his tense jaw, he meant it. *Okay. We're going all in.*

Cal hesitated, his eyes reflecting the battle between his fear and the desperate hope for closure. "I trusted Papa. I trust you. Please, Midas. Do what you can. If you find that you can't do anything, be honest with me. I know that you will."

Midas promised that he would do exactly that. Finally, nodding, Cal gave us his reluctant blessing. "One more night then," he conceded before turning away, leaving us to the shadows that now felt more oppressive, more animated than before.

Stepping into the building, the evidence of Cal's claims was undeniable.

The muddy footprints were everywhere. And it wasn't just one pair of feet. There were different sizes and shapes. It was an impossibility, a defiance of logic that chilled me to the core. On carpets that muffled our steps, across marble floors that gleamed dully in the weak light, even on walls and, most disturbingly, on ceilings.

It was as if the very essence of the tower had been corrupted, marked by a presence both unseen and unyielding.

It was then, amidst the chaos of our surroundings, that an inexplicable urge took hold of me. "I don't want to go up. Not yet. Let me just sit here, Midas," I murmured, almost afraid that my voice would shatter the fragile silence that enveloped us.

I didn't wait for his response, didn't see if he nodded or showed any sign of agreement. I simply found a spot, cleared it of the omnipresent mud, and sat, my sketchpad trembling in my hands. This compulsion to sketch, to draw, to share what I saw, it was hard to shake.

As my charcoal pencil touched the paper, it moved as if guided by a will that was not my own.

Faces began to emerge from the blankness, one after another, each bearing an expression that seemed to whisper secrets long buried within the tower's walls. Mostly elderly faces, probably the people that called this place home, but other faces came through too.

Children, infants, indigenous people. I half-sketched and then flipped the page and started again. With each stroke, a sense of urgency grew within me, a compulsion to keep drawing, to delve deeper into the unseen world that clung to the RSA Tower like a second skin.

The air in the RSA Tower felt heavier, as if saturated with unspoken stories and hidden truths, making each breath feel like a labor. Amidst the muddled chaos of muddy prints and whispered secrets, my hand moved with frenzied precision, sketching face after face, each a window to a soul long lost to the tower's embrace.

Sierra and Joshua, ever diligent in their quest for evidence, set up a static camera, its lens trained on me, capturing every stroke, every flicker of emotion that crossed my face. The sense of being watched, of being recorded, added an eerie layer of reality to the surreal task at hand. But they weren't the only ones watching.

The dead and the Man in Black were close by.

As I sketched, Macie came to sit beside me, her presence a silent pillar of support. The air around us felt charged, thick with the anticipation of revelation. My sketches took on a life of their own, leading me to a familiar face, one that whispered tales of sorrow and loss - Helene.

But as the charcoal traced her features, something shifted. The image morphed, my hand guided by an unseen force, flipping the pages in a desperate search for clarity, each turn a testament to the turmoil within me.

Then, amidst the emotional whirlwind, a scene unfolded on my pad - a heart-wrenching depiction of Sarah's tragic descent from the tower's roof. The image struck a chord, resonating with the eerie similarity to Jocelyn's fate at the Leaf Academy, her life snuffed out by a force as malevolent as the maelstrom that now seemed to engulf us.

As if I felt my hands were on fire, I slung the sketchpad down and stood up. I couldn't believe what just happened. I'd always tranced a bit when sketching or painting but this...this image was completely not one I would have ever drawn.

Macie's reaction was instantaneous, a mirror to the pain etched in the sketch.

Tears streamed down her face, a silent river of grief and empathy for the loss so vividly captured. The sketchbook, now a vessel of sorrow and revelation, lay forgotten as I reached out to her, our embrace a cocoon against the darkness that threatened to consume us.

"I'm so sorry, Macie. I didn't mean to draw this. I would never do this," I whispered, my voice a fragile thread in the dense tapestry of emotions that the night had woven. The moment was a poignant reminder of the raw, unspoken bonds that tethered us, a team united not just by the quest for the paranormal, but by the shared burden of the pain and loss it unearthed.

After witnessing my distress and Macie's reaction to the sketch, Midas stepped forward, his analytical mind piecing together the chilling implications. "This isn't just about hauntings," he murmured, more to himself than to the rest of us. "It's a message, and a very personal one."

His gaze locked with mine, seeking confirmation, understanding. With a heavy heart, I nodded, the truth of his words sinking in. The realization bound the team with a new determination, a shared resolve to confront whatever darkness awaited us.

We'd been pissing this thing off for two nights. This last night was for all the marbles.

We prepared to delve deeper into the tower's mysteries, armed with the knowledge that we were not just hunting ghosts, but confronting a narrative woven from pain and loss, directly challenging the malevolent presence we've come to know as the Man in Black.

Making several trips to the van, we gathered the rest of the gear. I offered to take samples of the mud, just for evidence's sake. Macie stuck close to me and I kept apologizing.

"Stop, Cassidy. It's not your fault. It's not anyone's fault, the maelstrom killed my sister. This thing, it read my mind. Read all our minds. As none of us are going to the roof, we're okay. Let's focus on samples and let's take lots of photographs.

For the next thirty minutes, we did just that. Instead of setting up the "brain room" on the fourth floor, we decided the lobby would work just fine. This thing, whatever it was, was not limited by the floors.

The silence that had enveloped the team as we worked, was shattered by a loud, resounding boom from the upper levels of the tower.

"Crap. So much for not going upstairs," Sierra announced.

The sound, so out of place in the quiet of the night, acted as a clarion call to action.

Without a word, the team gathered up their remaining equipment, their expressions a mix of fear and determination. Led by Midas, we headed for the elevators and ascended towards the source of the noise, each floor taking us deeper into danger.

The elevator door opened to the fourth floor. The air grew colder, the shadows darker, as if the building itself is reacting to their intrusion.

As we navigated the dimly lit corridors, the sense of being watched, of being followed, grew stronger. I could feel the eyes of the unseen on me, the weight of their gazes almost palpable. Our team moved with purpose, driven by a mix of professional duty and a personal quest for answers, bracing ourselves for whatever lay ahead.

Or so we thought.

The moment the elevator doors slid open, a shiver coursed through me, a prelude to the uncanny reality that greeted us on the fourth floor.

Despite the RSA Tower standing silent, the lights along the hallway flickered with a life of their own, casting erratic shadows that danced and twisted along the walls. It's as if the building itself breathed, mocking the very notion of abandonment.

The air was inexplicably colder here, a stark contrast to the mild night air we had left behind. Each breath we exhaled hung in front of us, a misty testament to the sudden drop in temperature.

I pulled my leather jacket tighter around me, but the cold wasn't just physical—it was a creeping chill that seemed to seep into my very bones, an ominous harbinger of what awaited.

Midas took the lead, his flashlight cut through the darkness, the beam a solid thing in the swirling mists that seemed to have appeared from nowhere. The rest of us followed closely, our own lights scanning the walls, the floor, the ceiling—anywhere that might offer a clue as to what's happening here.

The atmosphere was certainly charged, heavy with anticipation and an undercurrent of fear. It was not just the visible signs of the supernatural that unsettled me; it was the feeling of being watched, of unseen eyes tracking my every move.

"You feel that?" I asked no one in particular. The air felt thicker here, as if we were walking through a veil of unseen energy, a barrier between our world and another. Macie didn't answer but she nodded and held my hand. I was suddenly quite protective over her.

As we moved cautiously down the hallway, the lights continued their erratic dance, sometimes brightening to an almost blinding intensity before dimming to near darkness. It was disorienting, the constant shift between light and shadow, and it was deliberate, something—or someone—was manipulating the environment around us.

"We shouldn't be up here. Not tonight," Sierra whispered, her voice barely audible over the sound of our footsteps. I couldn't help but agree with her; every instinct screamed at us to turn back, to flee the oppressive atmosphere of the fourth floor. But we pushed forward, drawn by the need to understand, to confront whatever awaited us in the shadows.

It was not just the physical manifestations, the flickering lights, and the chilling cold. It was the sense of the malevolent intelligence behind it, a dark presence that seemed to be toying with us, leading us deeper into its domain.

We pressed on, the tension among us palpable. What lay ahead was unknown, but one thing was clear: we were not alone on this floor.

The supernatural forces at work in the RSA Tower were powerful, and they were aware of our presence. The question now is not if we will encounter them, but when—and what form that encounter will take.

As we continued our cautious advance, the eerie play of light and shadow seemed to intensify, the walls themselves appearing to pulse with an unseen heartbeat. The very fabric of reality felt distorted, as if we were walking through a dream—or a nightmare—crafted by the tower itself.

Suddenly, from the depths of the shadowed corridor, a sound broke the oppressive silence—a soft, mournful weeping that seemed to emanate from everywhere and nowhere.

It was a sound that tugged at the heart, filled with such sorrow and despair that it momentarily rooted us to the spot. The crying sounded so human, yet so far removed from anything living. It was a voice from the beyond, a sorrowful lament from the tower's tragic past.

Instinctively, we drew closer together, a collective response to the haunting sound.

Midas raised his hand and made a fist, signaling us to halt, his eyes scanning the darkness ahead. The weeping continued, a mournful soundtrack that seemed to grow in intensity, inviting us, or perhaps daring us, to delve deeper into the mystery.

With a shared glance that spoke volumes about our trepidation and determination, we decided to follow the sound. Each step took us further from the safety of the known, deeper into the heart of the tower's secrets. Each step we took I got the feeling that what we were hearing was not real.

The entity in this place was trying to trick us.

Then, as abruptly as it had begun, the weeping ceased, leaving a silence so complete it was as if the building itself was holding its breath.

"It's a trick," Joshua announced what we were all thinking. We paused, our own breathing loud in the sudden stillness, our lights casting about in search of the source of the cries. But there was nothing—only the empty hallway, its walls now silent, the shadows lying still.

It was in this silence, this moment of eerie calm, that we felt it—a sudden chill that swept through the corridor, so intense it felt as if the very air was being sucked from our lungs. And with it came a presence, a feeling of being watched by something ancient, something malevolent.

"He's here. I can feel him," I announced to the team. Sierra nodded in agreement. The sensation was overwhelming, a palpable pressure that seemed to press in on us from all sides.

Midas turned to us; his expression grim. "Be ready," he whispered, his voice barely audible. "It knows we're here."

Duh, I thought to myself.

And then, without warning, the shadows at the end of the hallway shifted, coalescing into a figure that was darker than the darkness itself.

"Midas! There!" Joshua shouted and it was then that I noticed he was wearing the RYDER helmet and Sierra was holding the tablet. She'd tapped the record button so everything was on film.

It was him—the Man in Black, his outline barely discernible, yet unmistakably present. He stood motionless, a sentinel of the shadows, watching us with an intensity that felt almost physical.

For a long moment, we simply stood there, locked in a silent standoff with this spectral figure, the air between us charged with an energy that was both terrifying and exhilarating.

Midas stood at the front of the group. "Why are you here?"

This was what we had come for, the confrontation with the unknown, the face-to-face with the supernatural.

Yet, even as we faced him, the Man in Black remained enigmatic, a figure of mystery and menace. He smiled, showing yellow teeth and he had an emaciated appearance.

What he wanted, why he haunted the RSA Tower, remained shrouded in darkness. But one thing was clear: this encounter was far from over.

The night was still young, and the tower's secrets lay deep. We had taken the first steps into its shadowy heart, but the path ahead promised only more questions, more mysteries, more danger.

With a deep breath, we prepared to move forward, to confront whatever lay ahead.

The Man in Black awaited, and we could not—would not—turn back now.

Chapter Thirteen–Jericho

As the night deepened around the RSA Tower, casting its ancient stones into silhouette against the moonlit sky, I found myself methodically considering the tools of our impending confrontation.

My hands, usually steady from years of both faith healing and handling delicate tech, trembled slightly with the weight of what lay ahead.

Inside my black investigative case, I knew a spectrum of devices blinked and hummed—their digital displays and sensors pierced the veil between worlds. I glanced up at Midas whose eyes widened.

"Open the case," he instructed, and I did as he asked. Sure enough, the K2 and other items were lit and firing off, even though no one had turned the power on. I closed it back up.

In my backpack, there were sacred objects laying in quiet testament to my heritage and faith: a cross passed down through generations, anointed oils whose scents mingled with the air, and a worn Bible, its pages filled with marginalia in my grandmother's careful handwriting.

"Jericho, you good?" Macie's voice, tinged with concern, cut through my reverie.

I looked up, offering her a smile that I hoped conveyed more confidence than I felt. "Yeah, Macie. Just making sure we're ready for whatever this entity throws at us."

Her hand found mine, squeezing gently, a silent message of support. We'd faced down darkness before, but something about tonight felt different—more final.

With the last of the preparations complete, I nodded to Midas, who had been watching from a respectful distance. "Let's do this," I said, my voice firm. "I'm ready. We need to follow him. He's trying to show us something."

We gathered in a semi-circle, the eclectic array of tools and sacred items between us, and began the initial phase of our plan to initiate contact. Sierra keyed up the static cameras, Joshua monitored the environmental sensors, and Cassidy, her eyes closed in concentration, reached out with her senses to provide a psychic beacon.

Almost immediately, the atmosphere shifted. "Alright, let's get ready. We'll follow him."

Screens flickered erratically, devices designed to measure, and record began to malfunction in ways that defied explanation, and a cold draft swept through the room, carrying with it the faint, unmistakable scent of brimstone.

"He's here," Cassidy whispered, her voice barely audible over the sudden surge of static that filled the air. "Still, and you're right. He wants us to follow him."

I took a deep breath, centering myself in the faith that had been my anchor through countless trials. "In the name of Jesus Christ, I command you to reveal yourself," I spoke into the charged air, my voice steady despite the chaos.

The response was immediate and visceral.

A howl, anguished and furious, echoed through the tower, sending a shiver down my spine. The temperature plummeted, and for a moment, the very fabric of reality seemed to thin, the veil between worlds growing tenuous.

"We're breaking through," I said, locking eyes with each member of the team. "Stay focused. We're in this together."

The entity's presence intensified, an oppressive force that seemed determined to push us back, to deny us any further progress. But we stood firm, united by purpose and bolstered by a resolve that was as much spiritual as it was born of our shared experiences.

This was just the beginning. The real confrontation lay ahead, and with it, the chance to uncover the truth hidden within the heart of the RSA Tower.

The howl of the entity reverberated through the tower, a sound that seemed to come from the very walls themselves. As we stood, resolute in the face of this unseen aggression, a memory flickered to the forefront of my mind—a moment of calm in my grandmother's kitchen, her voice steady and sure as she imparted a piece of advice that had stuck with me through the years.

"Jericho," she had said, her eyes locking with mine, "there's power in the Word, and there's power in your faith. When you face darkness, remember this," she had handed me a slip of paper, "it's been in our family for generations, a prayer of protection and strength."

Now, with my team's eyes on me, I felt the weight of that memory, the responsibility of carrying forward that legacy. I reached into my pocket, feeling the worn edges of the paper, and pulled it out. The words, penned in my grandmother's elegant script, shimmered in the dim light as I began to recite them aloud.

"Lord, Your Word says, 'No weapon formed against us shall prosper.' I stand on that promise as we confront this darkness..."

As I spoke, a warmth spread through me, an affirmation of my faith and my purpose. The oppressive air lightened momentarily, the entity's howls dimming as if repelled by the sheer force of belief.

The team's stance shifted, shoulders relaxing slightly, bolstered by the invocation. But we couldn't relax too much. There was still a battle ahead of us.

The moment of calm provided us with the opportunity to press forward, and as we did, the tower seemed to shift around us, corridors twisting until we found ourselves before a heavy, unmarked door that hadn't been there before.

Or at least we hadn't seen it before. There was nothing to mark it significantly except for a narrow sign next to the door. With a collective breath, we pushed it open, revealing the hidden chapel beyond.

The contrast was stark.

Here, within these sacred walls, the air was calm, almost reverent. The chapel was a mosaic of faiths, a testament to the tower's diverse present. The statue of the Virgin Mary stood alongside a candle stand; I could imagine its flames flickering in silent prayer.

Protestant hymnals lay neatly stacked beside a worn wooden pulpit, while across the room, Islamic calligraphy adorned the walls, a beautiful, intricate pattern that spoke of devotion and peace.

"Trippy," Macie said as she usually did when she didn't know what else to say. "I've never been in a place like this. What would you call it? A Universalist Church? A multi-cultural center?"

"I'm not sure," Midas answered quietly as he took measurements with his EMF reader. "Readings are high in here. Oh no. Look at this. The temp is dropping." I glanced over his shoulder, not quite surprised to see the numbers 66.6 show up.

The entity was certainly making his presence known.

It was a sanctuary, a place where all were welcome, a melting pot of beliefs unified in their search for solace and connection with the divine. Or at least their choice of the divine.

Here, in this chapel, the divisions of the outside world seemed trivial, the shared human yearning for understanding and peace the only truth that mattered.

As we focused on examining the space, the door swung shut behind us with a soft click, sealing us within the tranquility of the chapel. The rage of the Man in Black felt stronger here, his power seemingly made stronger by the unusual religious center. This chapel, with its eclectic symbols of faith, was a reminder of the tower's capacity for light amidst the darkness, a beacon of hope in our quest.

Yet, as serene as the chapel was, we knew that our confrontation was far from over.

The Man in Black's rage was palpable, a storm brewing on the horizon. But for now, we stood together in the eye of that storm, ready for whatever lay ahead, fortified by the chapel's peace and the strength drawn from our diverse beliefs.

Suddenly, without warning, the tranquil scene before us descended into chaos. Prayer candles that had not been lit, flickering gently moments before flaring to life with an intensity that defied the natural order, casting grotesque shadows that danced along the walls with a life of their own.

"Crap! Where's the fire extinguisher?" I demanded but nobody had answers. Too much was happening, too quickly.

Hymnals and sacred texts, once neatly stacked, levitated before being hurled across the room with force enough to shatter the silence with the sound of tearing pages.

The pulpit, that symbol of spiritual guidance and faith, began to shake, its ancient wood groaning under an unseen force. And then, as if in response to an unspoken command, it splintered, fragments of wood suspended in the air before scattering like leaves in a tempest.

From the corners of the room, the statues and icons of faith seemed to weep, tears of oil bleeding down their sacred forms, while the Islamic calligraphy on the walls shimmered as if alive, reacting to the presence that invaded this holy place.

Above the cacophony, an otherworldly roar filled the chapel, a sound so deep and so full of hatred it felt as though the very air might tear apart.

"Midas!" Cassidy shouted as she clutched her husband's arm. There was no time to run.

The Man in Black with the funny hat, his fury manifesting in a tangible wave of darkness that swept through the chapel, extinguishing the candles and plunging us into darkness save for the eerie glow of our own devices, flickering uncertainly in the oppressive gloom.

The chapel, once a place of refuge, had become the battleground for our confrontation with the Man in Black. His power was palpable, a pressure against every sense that screamed for us to flee, to abandon this place of consecrated ground now profaned by his rage.

But we did not.

For amidst the terror, a fire kindled within me, fueled by the faith and the love of those who stood with me. We had come to confront the darkness, not to be turned away by it.

"He hates this place. You hate it, don't you?" I shouted at him. Now I was catching on. A disembodied growl filled the sacred room. Everyone heard it. Midas nodded his approval while I kept going. Macie stood beside me, ready to help however she could. Sierra was watching the tablet but Joshua was still wearing the RYDER helmet.

"I see him, Jericho. Here's right there. Behind where the pulpit used to be. Oh geesh, my head is killing me. What the..." Joshua snatched off RYDER and closed his eyes. Sierra took it from him and returned it to its case.

"I recorded everything, Joshua. That's enough of that helmet."

"She's right, Josh. I can see him. Macie, use the holy water, sprinkle it in front of the door. We can't let him leave. This needs to end tonight."

In the midst of turmoil, amidst the swirling chaos that had overtaken the chapel, a sense of purpose steadied my heart. I stepped forward, the fragments of the shattered pulpit crunching underfoot, and began to lay out the items we had brought with us—each a symbol of faith, each a testament to the power of belief in the face of darkness.

Around me, my team rallied, their faces set in determined lines, ready to support the ritual that was to come.

I started with the simple act of lighting a candle, its flame a beacon of hope amidst the shadows.

One by one, the team joined in, lighting candles using the flame from mine, until the chapel was filled with points of light, pushing back against the darkness that sought to envelop us.

"Lord, in Your mercy, hear our prayer," I began, my voice steady. The words of the ritual were a blend of the faiths represented in the chapel, a call to unity in the face of division, to strength in the face of fear.

As I spoke, the air grew warmer, the oppressive chill pushed back by the collective force of our belief.

Macie, at my side, began to sing, her voice lifting in a familiar hymn, *Amazing Grace,* that seemed to fill the chapel with light. Sierra joined in, her voice harmonizing with Macie's, while Joshua and Cassidy added their own voices to the melody.

The sound was pure, a prayer, and as it rose, the shadows seemed to recoil, the Man in Black's presence wavering under the assault of our combined faith. He roared in anger. He fluttered in and out of vision.

It was like watching a hologram, an odd hologram. Like one you would see in an old science fiction movie.

And then, in the midst of the ritual, a silence fell. It was as if the very air held its breath, and in that silence, we saw him—the Man in Black, his form clearer now, less a shadow and more a man, his eyes filled with an unspeakable hatred.

"You cannot stay here," I whispered, the words not just a command, but a plea. "Let us help you find peace."

"There is no peace! This is evil!"

The candles flickered as if caught in a sudden breeze, and the Man in Black's form shimmered, the edges of his presence blurring as if he was struggling to maintain his shape.

It was working; the ritual, the unity of our faiths, was reaching him, touching something deep within the torment that had drawn him to this place. "Tell me your name! Who are you? If you tell me your name, I can help you. We can help you!"

Suddenly Macie spoke but her voice was strange, solemn, trancelike. "It won't do you any good. He has no name."

She stared in front of her, as if she could see something we could not. Clearly, she did, at first. Then he manifested himself into something entirely different. The Man in Black was no longer a man in a tri-cornered hat but a tall being, extremely tall. His bones cracked as he became something horrible. Tall, lanky arms, long legs, black reptilian skin and piercing yellow eyes.

"I know your name," I said as I held my ground and resisted the urge to challenge him directly. "You are no demon, but you are unholy. I know, I've met you before. You stand in the way of God's work. You are carnal and cruel. You are self-righteousness, but we will call you what you are, a Spirit of Religion!"

As my words echoed through the charged air of the chapel, a cold shiver ran down my spine. The atmosphere thickened, heavy with a foreboding silence that seemed to warp the very fabric of reality around us.

Shadows pooled and swirled at a focal point in the room, congregating into a dense mass from which the figure of Religion emerged, his presence a tangible weight upon our chests.

"Religion..." I whispered, the name tasting like ash on my tongue. As the word unfurled into the shadow-laden air, a palpable shift occurred. The Man in Black—Religion—froze, his form momentarily wavering as if the name had invoked a power he had long feared. Why had I doubted myself? Of course this was the spirit of Religion.

"Your name is Religion," I asserted, the pieces of the enigma intertwining into a grim tapestry. This entity, this harbinger of despair within the RSA Tower, was intrinsically tied to the dichotomy of faith—a beacon of hope ensnared in the web of division and sorrow.

Acknowledging his true name caused Religion's visage to solidify from the shadows, manifesting into a ghastly specter of malevolence. His eyes ignited with a sinister flame, piercing through the dim light of the chapel with a hatred that threatened to engulf us in its inferno.

"You know nothing," he spat, his voice a symphony of discordant whispers that clawed at our minds, dripping with venomous intent. "You do not know my power. Let me show you!"

In an instant, the entity known as Religion launched himself towards us, a phantasmagoric blur propelled by centuries of suppressed rage.

Sierra, caught in the path of his fury and too engrossed in her documentation of the moment, was rendered defenseless. She was struck with a force that seemed to emanate from the abyss itself, her petite form careening through the air before collapsing to the ground, the tablet skittering across the marble floor like a stone across a pond.

"Sierra Kay!" Joshua screamed as he ran to her side.

The impact resonated through the chapel, a stark reminder of the power wielded by the entity before us. The air was expelled from Sierra's lungs in a visible plume, her body crumpled in a heap of vulnerability.

The chapel, a sanctuary of diverse faiths, now bore witness to a confrontation as ancient as belief itself.

Religion, now fully revealed in his horrific glory, towered before us, a specter of the twisted sanctity he represented. His form was a tapestry of darkness, woven from the countless souls ensnared by his wrath, his eyes gleaming with a malevolence born of untold millennia.

"Leave or I will take her!" The thing said in a crackling, devilish voice.

Panic surged. "No! Sierra!" I shouted, rushing to her side. Her fall seemed to break the momentary spell that had held us all captive, spurring the team into action. Joshua and Cassidy moved to form a barrier between us and Religion, while Macie knelt beside Sierra, checking for injuries.

The entity, Religion, hovered near, his form pulsating with dark energy, clearly readying for another attack. But something had shifted with the revelation of his name; the power dynamics in the room felt different, as if calling him by name had given us a measure of control.

"We command you, Religion—in the name of all that is holy and just, to cease your torment," I declared, standing to face him, my team beside me. "You are bound by the truths of faith, Religion, by the hope and unity it's supposed to inspire, not the division and fear you've sown."

Religion recoiled as if struck, his form flickering. "Impossible," he growled, but there was a note of uncertainty in his voice now, a crack in the facade that had seemed impenetrable moments before. "You have no power here! You cannot defeat me!"

The chapel, filled with symbols of faith from across the spectrum of human belief, seemed to resonate with our declaration, the sacred items glowing softly with an inner light. It was as if the very essence of the chapel was lending us its strength, bolstering our stand against the darkness.

Sierra, recovering, pushed herself up with Macie's help, her gaze locked on Religion.

Sierra's declaration cut through the tension like a blade, her voice a beacon of defiance in the shadow-clad chapel. "Your reign here is over. You will no longer use the guise of faith to spread your malice. I know what you did to Helene! I know what you did!"

Her words seemed to hang in the air, charged with a power that transcended mere sound, resonating with the very stones of the sacred space.

In response, Religion's howl tore through the chapel, a sound so filled with rage and despair that it seemed to claw at the very fabric of reality. The air itself vibrated with the force of his fury, a maelstrom of darkness that threatened to engulf us in its tempest.

But as his scream reached its crescendo, something miraculous occurred.

His form, once a solid mass of shadow and malevolence, began to fracture, the darkness that made up his being starting to unravel as if caught in an unseen gale. It was as though the holy words, the invocation, I had spoken had unleashed a power capable of tearing him apart from the inside, the truth of the declaration acting as a catalyst for his undoing.

We stood, a tight-knit circle of light amidst the encroaching darkness, watching in a mix of horror and fascination as the entity known as Religion was unmade before our eyes.

His once formidable shape dissolved, shadows peeling away from him like the pages of a burned book, each strip curling into nothingness as it was consumed by an invisible flame.

The process was terrifying, a visual testament to the battle between light and shadow playing out before us. The chapel, once a place of serene sanctuary, now echoed with the sounds of this unseen battle, the air thick with the scent of ozone as if the very atmosphere was being torn asunder.

As the last of Religion's form disintegrated, a final, guttural roar of defiance bellowed from the void where he had stood, a sound so laden with hatred and sorrow that it chilled us to our bones.

It was a sound that spoke of battles fought and lost, of centuries of twisted existence finally coming to an end.

And then, silence. The chapel, now free from the presence that had so long haunted it, seemed to breathe a sigh of relief, the oppressive atmosphere lifting as if a great weight had been removed. The darkness receded, and for the first time in what felt like an eternity, the air felt clean, purged of the malevolence that had dominated it.

We looked around, the remnants of our ordeal settling around us like dust. The echo of Religion's final cry lingered in the air, a haunting reminder of the entity that had once claimed dominion over this place. But now, nothing remained of him but the memory of his fury and the legacy of darkness he had left behind.

The chapel fell silent, the oppressive atmosphere that had marked Religion's presence evaporating like mist in the morning sun. We exchanged looks of relief and disbelief, the tension of the night's events giving way to a profound sense of peace.

I prayed the battle was over but that's when I spotted Sierra laying on the floor.

Chapter Fourteen—Helene

In the dim light of our modest colonial home, I faced Francis, my heart sinking as I saw the resolve in his eyes waver—not with doubt over what he believed, but over what he feared from our neighbors. The very fabric of our life together seemed to unravel as the truth of his betrayal became clear to me.

What did he expect me to do? How could he ask this of me?

"Francis, please," I begged, my voice a whisper of despair, "you know the peril that awaits me if they find out. We must leave, or at the very least, send me back home where I can live and practice my faith in peace."

My hands instinctively went to my belly, the life within me a testament to our shared love and now, a shared danger.

He paced the room, a man torn between the love for his wife and the invisible chains of societal norms that held him fast. *How could he not protect me? How could he not protect our child? Has everything he promised me been a lie?*

"Helene, sweetheart," he started, his voice strained, "you must understand, the colony...they will not tolerate your...our beliefs. It is not just you in danger; it is us, our family, our child. I am shocked at their intolerance, but I worry that I will not be able to protect us—protect you."

I couldn't believe what I was hearing. Was this the man I married? It seemed I'd stepped into some sort of nightmare. The man who vowed to stand by me through all trials, who knew of my faith when he took me as his wife, who celebrated it in the privacy of our home?

"You knew what I believed, husband. You assured my family that you would care for me! You are a Protestant as am I, and yet you brought me here," I said, the weight of my disbelief anchoring each word. "Why? To die? You can't let them do this, Francis. Please, you must protect us. The child, me!"

How many times had I had to hide in the swamp? How many times had I fled their anger? Yet my handsome husband, with his good looks and apparently no backbone would not help me.

His gaze met mine, and in his brown eyes, I saw the tumultuous sea of his fears. Fear for our safety, yes, but also fear of the repercussions from the colony, fear of the isolation that defying them would bring. It was a fear that clouded his judgment and steeled his resolve against me.

"I...I cannot, Helene," he finally admitted, his voice barely a whisper, betraying the inner battle he fought. "The colony, the priest...they would never allow us to live in peace. It is too late. I have already made my pledge to the Catholic church. This is the way it must be, Helene."

Too late.

The words echoed in my mind, a death knell for the life I had envisioned for us, for our child. In that moment, I realized the full extent of Francis's betrayal. Not just of our vows, but of the very essence of who we were together. He had chosen the path of least resistance, at the cost of everything we held dear.

Francis was lost to me, swallowed by the fear that governed the hearts of men. And with him, my last hope for salvation in this new world vanished like smoke in the wind.

The ominous murmur of voices outside grew louder, an angry tide rising against the frail barricade of our home. Through the window, I glimpsed torches flickering like malevolent stars against the night sky, each flame a harbinger of the coming storm.

Where were the servants? They too had fled. They weren't fools. I should have fled with them. Living in the wilderness could not be worse than what I was facing.

The pounding on the door started soon after, each thud a heavy blow to my already sinking heart. "Helene Dagurette! We demand to speak with thee!" they shouted, their voices a tangled mess of anger and righteousness. "Bring out the heretic!"

The priest's voice, venomous and piercing, rose above the rest, condemning my teachings and my faith. The fear inside me twisted, knotted tightly with dread and disbelief. How could this be happening?

Francis's face was pale, his eyes darting between the door and me, the resolve that had once held some hint of protection now crumbling visibly.

"No! Francis! You cannot let them in!"

"Helene, I..." he started, his voice a tremulous whisper, but the clamor outside swallowed his words. "We have to face this." With a shaking hand, he unlatched the door.

My heart screamed in protest, a silent plea that went unheeded. As the door swung open, revealing the hateful faces of the mob, Francis stepped back, his place by my side abandoned.

"Please, do not hurt my wife," he muttered weakly to the priest, his plea for my safety feeble and fleeting. But his words fell on deaf ears, or perhaps on hearts too hardened by fervor to care.

"If she comes to her senses, if she abandons her heresy, we are prepared to leave her in peace. Is that what she wishes to do? Rather than contaminate the servants and slaves with her heretical teaching?"

"Heretical teaching?" I repeated stupidly.

The room spun around me, the faces of my accusers blurring into a nightmare from which there was no waking.

Francis's betrayal was complete, the man I loved, the father of my child, had delivered me into the hands of my persecutors. His final, faltering attempt to plead for me did nothing to stem the tide of betrayal that washed over me, leaving me cold and alone in its wake.

As the mob's rough hands seized me, pulling me from the threshold of what had once been my sanctuary, my mind reeled in shock and horror. Each step away from my home felt like a descent into some dark abyss from which there was no return.

"Francis, please, don't let them do this!" I cried out, my voice cracking under the strain of terror and desperation. But my plea was lost in the roar of accusations and condemnations thrown at me. Mrs. Dewitt spit on me while other hands pinched and tugged at my flesh and my dress.

The grip on my arms tightened, dragging me forward, each step punctuated by my growing despair. Inside, a fierce battle raged—fear for the tiny life growing within me battling against the cold realization of my husband's betrayal.

How could Francis who had once promised to shield me from the world's cruelties stand by and watch as I was torn away from him?

My faith, which had always been my fortress, now seemed like the very thing that would lead me to my ruin. Yet, it was that same faith that I clung to, a beacon in the storm, urging me to remain steadfast, even as tears blurred my vision and my heart threatened to break under the weight of my sorrows.

Through the blur of my tears, I saw Francis standing in the doorway of our whitewashed home, his figure a distant, wavering shadow. He seemed smaller somehow, diminished by his own indecision and fear. The expressions flitting across his face told the story of a man torn apart by his own failings. Guilt, shame, and fear danced in his eyes, each emotion taking its turn as he watched me being pulled further and further away.

"Franics, please! Don't do this. Not if you love me!"

I could almost hear his thoughts, the tumultuous whirl of self-reproach and terror that kept him rooted to the spot, unable to come to my aid.

His voice, once firm and comforting, now seemed like a distant echo, "I am sorry, Helene. It is the will of the colony, of the people, of our neighbors," he murmured, too low for anyone but himself to hear. His apology, muffled by the distance and the chaos around me, did nothing to ease the pain. It was a feeble whisper, lost in the wind, as if he believed those feeble words could absolve him of his inaction.

The sight of him, so paralyzed by his own fears, was the final betrayal, the ultimate letdown from the man I had once loved unconditionally. I had been a seventeen-year-old fool to marry such a man. Mother warned me, encouraged me to wait, to stay at home but I had not listened to her wisdom.

As I was dragged away to the city square, Francis' figure receded into the background, just another shadow among the many, fading into the dark tapestry of my forsaken life.

Dragged into the city square, the mob's fury was a palpable force, pressing in from all sides. They forced me to my knees in front of the sweaty, fat priest, a man whose face was twisted with zealotry.

His voice boomed over the crowd, demanding that I renounce my Protestant faith and accept their doctrine as my own. "You are walking dangerously close to witchcraft, Helen Dagurette. Renounce your faith and pledge allegiance to the true faith."

My limbs trembled, not from fear of my fate but from the force of my resolve. "I am no witch but a God fearing woman! I will not renounce my faith," I declared, my voice stronger than I felt. It carried across the murmuring crowd, a defiant echo in the oppressive air. "I will not abandon my faith for anyone. Not for you, or Franics, or any of you."

To my surprise, Francis's face appeared in the sea of hostile faces, his eyes pleading with me to yield, to save myself. "Helene! Please, listen to Father Jerome."

But to renounce my faith would be to betray my very soul. "I am steadfast in my belief. I will not renounce what I believe." I told the priest, even as his followers began their brutal chastisement.

Blows rained down upon me—fists and feet and spit. I could hear Francis pleading for them to stop but he did nothing more. The pain was immense, but it was his betrayal that hurt more profoundly. A call for a blade cut through the chaos, a deadly whisper that promised an end.

My vision blurred with blood and tears, the figures around me morphing into dark shadows against the harsh light of the torches. I could taste blood in my mouth, my lip was busted and I was pretty sure I'd lost a tooth.

As the physical assault waned, my body bruised and broken, my mind found clarity in the face of impending death. Thoughts of my unborn child filled me with a profound sadness for the life we would not share, for the world they would never see.

"Think of the innocent child, Helene. Renounce Protestantism. Call on Mother Mary and make your peace. Do this and we will allow you to live. Allow you to return to your home." Jerome's fetid breath sickened me.

Yet, even as despair threatened to overwhelm me, my love for Francis, tangled though it was with betrayal, brought a bitter comfort. He had loved me, in his way, and perhaps in another life, it would have been enough. But not in this one. My life was soon to be over.

Somehow, I found a way to kneel on my bruised knees. I could feel the blood flowing between my legs. I would lose my child, but not before I lost my life. We would die together.

I began to pray, the words of the Lord's Prayer a soothing balm on my battered spirit. "Our Father, who art in heaven, hallowed by thy name..." I spoke through swollen lips, each word a step closer to peace.

The voices around me faded to a distant hum, the pain became a distant ache, and as I spoke the final words of the prayer, darkness crept into the edges of my vision, a gentle, encroaching night. I glanced up at the night sky, the stars bright and twinkling above as if all was well in the world. It was not.

"Thy kingdom come..." were the last words I knew before the world went dark, a serene silence enveloping me in its final embrace.

My spirit, unbroken by the trials I had endured, soared beyond the confines of mortal pain and betrayal, carried aloft by an unshakeable faith and a heart, though broken, still full of love.

"Helene!" I heard my husband scream as the world began to spin. No. My head spun from my body, the blade at least had done its dirty work with one stroke.

I was no more.

Chapter Fifteen—Sierra

I shuddered back to the present, my vision clearing as the echo of ancient chants faded into the swirling mist of Mobile's wooded outskirts. The memory of Helene's horrible last moments lingered and I realized I was inside, not in the town square. The oppressive atmosphere of the land clawed at my senses, thick with the residue of a cursed past.

I felt Joshua's steadying hand on my shoulder, his presence a brief solace against the cold dread that clung to my skin. "Joshua, thank God it's you."

"It's okay, Sierra," he whispered, his voice low and concerned. He helped me to my feet as I wiped away tears that had spilled over for Helene. In that flashback, through the eyes of someone long gone, I had witnessed a sacrilegious ceremony that twisted the very spirit of the land.

This was not merely a ghost story; it was a tragedy of the highest order.

Jericho, who had been quietly observing the surrounding area, nodded gravely. "Also known as a Python Spirit, or the Jezebel Spirit," he added. "It was an ancient force, one that preys on faith and twists it into something dark. It's what makes a church a cult, it distorts faith. I think the multi-faith chapel set it off."

I nodded in agreement. "This spirit has made Mobile its home," I continued, feeling a chill as the words left my lips. The idea that such malevolence could lurk in the shadows of our everyday lives was unnerving. "There's no way we can cast a spirit out of a whole city."

Big Brother spoke up. "That's not the assignment, Sierra Kay. Let's just clear this building, the grounds. That's all we can do. Which leaves us with Francis. He's still here."

My skin crawled at hearing that but I knew it was true. Bound by guilt. Bound by cowardice.

Joshua squeezed my shoulder reassuringly, his eyes scanning the hallway around us as if expecting the spirit to materialize from the shadows. "We'll find a way to deal with this," he said, more to himself than to me.

As the last whispers of the flashback echoed in my mind, a deeper, more sinister revelation surfaced. The spirit, a corrupt religious entity, had not only claimed the land but had also claimed lives.

Blood and betrayal were in the foundations, sowing seeds of malevolence that stretched far beyond the forgotten pages of history. And Helene, poor Helene, her murder had been a sacrifice to this spirit's insatiable hunger.

Forgotten by the world, her spirit was bound to the cursed land, a pawn in a game that began centuries ago. Her tragic spirit summoned by the Religious Spirit. Still tormenting her.

The weight of what we faced settled heavily upon us. It was more than a haunting; it was a fight against a darkness that had roots deeper than the ancient oaks that stood as silent witnesses to Helene's demise.

I wasn't sure what the next steps would be but as we were reviewing the footage on our portable monitors a tall, lanky figure flickered into view on the upper floor's camera feed. His outline was murky, but there was no mistaking the shape of him.

"There!" I pointed. "He's inside. He's on the second floor. That's Francis. His features aren't clear, but I think that's him!"

Grabbing our gear, we headed towards the staircase, the echo of our steps a sharp contrast to the hush that filled the air. Forget the elevator. We might get stuck in there.

As we ascended the steps, the air grew noticeably colder, a tangible reminder of the spirit's power. We did not have to search for him. We found the entity standing by a window, the light casting long shadows across his form.

It appeared to be Francis—or at least, it wore his face. His eyes, were voids of sorrow, lacking warmth and recognition that characterized the man I'd seen in my vision. The man that poor Helene had loved, to her great consternation.

"It's Francis but remember, he's been under the influence of the evil entity for centuries," I whispered to the team, my voice barely audible. The wrongness of his aura was palpable, a stark perversion of the human soul it had overshadowed.

The figure turned to face us as we approached, his lips curling into a semblance of a smile. "Why have you come, witch?" it asked, its voice eerily mimicking Francis's timbre. Clearly it was speaking to me.

I flinched, the familiar sound of his voice clashing with the dark energy that radiated from him. Internally, I wrestled with doubt. Was there any part of the real Francis left in there? Could there be a fragment of his spirit still fighting for dominance within?

Jericho stepped forward, his posture firm and authoritative. "We've come to end this," he declared, his voice resonant with the power of his faith. "We want to help you, Francis Dagurette. We can help you."

As an ordained holy man, Jericho was no stranger to spiritual warfare, and his presence brought a measure of confidence to our shaken group.

The dead man frowned, a sight that chilled me to the bone. "You think you can banish me so easily?" it taunted, the room seeming to darken with its challenge. "Stronger men than you have tried."

Jericho began to pray softly, his words a mix of invocation and command.

As he did so, the entity's form flickered, briefly revealing glimpses of the spirit's true, horrifying visage. But somehow, I knew that Francis was trapped too. Trapped in the clutches of the entity that faced us. Even though the entity had been evicted from the property, it didn't seem to want to give up Francis.

Jericho's voice grew more insistent as he reached into his satchel, pulling out an assortment of sacred objects—a crucifix, holy water, and an old, leather-bound Bible that looked as if it had been through wars.

"Everyone take something. Whatever your faith, pray. Whatever you believe, believe it with all your might."

Each of us armed with a symbol of faith, formed a tight circle around Francis. "With these items," Jericho continued, "we weaken your hold, we break the chains binding you to this land, and we free Francis from your grip. Let him go. He is of no use to you anymore."

The plan was desperate, hinging on our unity and the potency of the sacred objects we held. As Jericho began to chant—a deep, resonant prayer that seemed to vibrate through the floorboards—the air around us charged, as if anticipating a storm.

No sooner had Jericho's voice risen in a crescendo of faith than the environment responded. A cold wind swept through the room, strangely enough, it drained the batteries of the digital recorder and the handheld camera that Midas was using.

The shadows around us grew longer, more menacing, as if they were alive, twisting and writhing against the walls.

Temperatures plummeted, breaths turned to mist in the chilling air, and a dense, eerie fog began to seep through the cracks in the floorboards, enveloping the second floor in a ghostly shroud. The atmosphere was charged with a malevolent energy, a clear signal that the spirit was not only aware of our intentions but was fiercely opposing them.

Suddenly, from the mist, Hyram's figure emerged, his face pale and eyes wide with terror. "He's going to get angry again," he gasped, his voice barely audible over the howling wind that now filled the building. "It's not safe for you here!"

"Run, hide somewhere safe!" I shouted to the ghost, over the roar, pointing towards the staircase. Without hesitation, Hyram nodded, disappearing into a wall but his footsteps echoing in the tumultuous atmosphere.

As he disappeared, the entity's smile widened, a grotesque mimicry of amusement. "Is that fear I smell?" it taunted, its voice a horrifying blend of Francis's tone and something far older, far darker. Had I been wrong? Had the spirit of Religion successfully fused itself to the dead man?

We tightened our circle, the sacred objects in our hands our only defense against the dark power that seemed to press in from all sides. The chill was bone-deep, and the fog swirled more aggressively, as if driven by the spirit's wrath.

Jericho's prayers grew louder, more urgent, his words slicing through the darkness.

It was a battle of wills on a field that felt as ancient as time itself, and we were in the heart of it, fighting not just for Francis but for our own souls.

With no time left to hesitate, I urged the gather in the fourth floor hallway, the chilling presence of the entity propelling us to move quickly. As we spread out, placing the sacred objects in a circle around us, the spirit's wrath became tangible. The air thickened, pulsing with malice, and the ground beneath our feet seemed to tremble with latent anger. Hallucinations began to manifest around us—shadowy figures darting up and down the hallways.

"Don't listen to them!" I shouted, my voice barely cutting through the cacophony of ghostly murmurs. "Focus on the task!" But even as I spoke, I could see the strain on my teammates' faces, their eyes darting nervously, fighting the urge to succumb to the spectral manipulations.

Still clutching the various holy objects, a violent shudder ran through the building. The structure groaned ominously, as if the very foundations were protesting our intrusion. Midas, ever the pragmatist, surveyed the escalating danger with a critical eye.

"We need more time! He won't let us help him," he declared firmly, his voice cutting through the escalating terror. "Let's get out of here!" His decision, made with the authority of experience, was irrevocable. The risk had become too great; the spirit was too powerful, and our safety was now in jeopardy.

Francis laughed at us but he had vanished, leaving behind a horrible smell. This wasn't over but Midas was correct. It was too dangerous right now, not to mention that there was a full moon tonight. Never good for paranormal investigations.

We gathered our gear with hands that trembled not just from the cold but from the fear that clung to us like a second skin. As we hurriedly packed, the sounds of the building settling around us seemed more sinister, like the spirit itself was trying to bring down the walls upon us.

"Is he going to tear it down?" Macie asked fearfully. "With us inside it?"

Jericho soothed her fears. "Let's just get out of here." And we did just that. Down one set of stairs and then another.

Once outside, the tower loomed larger somehow, its shadows deeper and more threatening. The land around us felt alive with hostility, the trees swaying without wind, their branches clawing at the darkening sky as if trying to pull us back.

With every step we took away from that cursed tower, the oppressive weight of the land pressed closer, as if the spirit sought to trap us forever within its grasp. We moved quickly, almost running, our breaths visible in the frigid air and our hearts pounding with the urgent need to escape.

It was not just a retreat; it was a flight from an ancient evil that had no intention of letting go easily. The boundary of the property was in sight, yet it seemed to recede with every step we took, the nightmare of the place clinging to us, unwilling to release its hold.

Midas's voice cut sharply through the heavy air as we reached the van, parked ominously under the gnarled branches of an old oak.

"Everyone, get in! It's time to go! We got what we came for." His tone left no room for argument, and one by one, we piled into the vehicle, the interior offering a stark contrast to the chill and dread outside.

Inside the van, a collective sigh of relief washed over us, the safety of the enclosed space allowing our adrenaline to ebb slightly. But as my teammates began to relax, my thoughts were haunted by the vision of Helene, the woman whose tragic fate had led us to this haunted place.

Tears streamed down my cheeks, unchecked and warm against the coldness that had seeped into my bones. I couldn't shake the image of Helene—her face and hands dirtied from the struggle of her last moments, her expression imbued with an eternal sadness and hopelessness. I could feel Macie and Cassidy's sympathetic hands on my shoulders and I thanked them for it.

As the van pulled away, I turned for one last look at the tower.

There, amidst the thickening fog and deepening twilight, stood Helene. She was dressed in her 18th-century attire, the fabric of her dress fluttering slightly as if caught in a breeze that touched only her. Our eyes met across the distance, her gaze piercing through the veil of time and sorrow.

I am sorry, Helene. I am sorry for what happened to you.

Her presence was a silent plea, a reminder that our departure was a respite, not a resolution. The tower, with its foreboding silhouette against the night sky, seemed to shrink back into the landscape as we drove away, but the memory of Helene remained, vivid and haunting.

Please, help him! I told no one what she asked of me.

The van's engine hummed a low, steady rhythm as we made our way back to civilization, the normalcy of the road a stark contrast to the supernatural battleground we had just fled.

My teammates chatted quietly, their voices a murmur against the sound of the road, but I sat in silence, Helene's despairing image etched into my mind, a solemn vow that I would return, that we would find a way to free her spirit from the chains of her tormentor.

As the lights of downtown Mobile came into view, the shadow of the tower and its spectral inhabitants seemed like a dark dream fading at dawn.

Yet the resolve in my heart was clear—this was only the beginning of our battle, not the end.

Helene and Francis would be free, or I would die trying.

Chapter Sixteen–Midas

The first light of dawn had barely broken over the horizon when I awoke, the lingering shadows of last night's horrors still clutching at the fringes of my mind. Despite the weight of exhaustion that pressed heavily upon my shoulders, a spark of determination kindled within me—a silent vow to set things right, to free Helene and break the dark hold on Francis.

I loved my job but after nights like last night, I felt old. Tired and old.

As I lay there, contemplating the day ahead, the soft stirrings of my son, Dominic, pulled me back to a gentler reality. I could hear him babbling over the baby monitor.

Cassidy was still sleeping, the fatigue of our endless nights evident on her beautiful, peaceful face. I slipped out of bed quietly, my joints protesting slightly, and headed down the hall to the nursery. My son smiled up at me. I scooped Dominic into my arms and immediately realized he needed to be changed.

"Ugh, son. What a way to start the day. You smell. You're a smelly boy, Dominic Demopolis." The cat poked his black furry head in the door but didn't come in. I could tell by the look on his face that he thought that smell was too much for him too.

I quickly changed his bottom and my little guy gurgled happily as we headed to the kitchen. I prepared his breakfast, his bright eyes watching every move I made with curiosity. We chatted or rather I chatted and he blabbered about his Cheerios. I could tell he had plenty to say but wasn't quite able to say what was on his mind. But he was getting better at saying Daddy, that was all that mattered.

My cell phone was dinging, I could see from here it was my aunt, but I wasn't ready to deal with today's challenges. I never wanted Papa Angelos's job. That honor should have gone to my great aunt. Screw tradition. Aunt Wilda was more than capable of taking care of the family business matters.

Strangely enough, she was the one that resisted this idea the most. Her and my father and there was no way I was giving him access to the Demopolis checkbook. Not a chance in hell.

Cassidy joined us shortly, her steps soft against the wooden floor. She'd piled her auburn curls on top of her head in a messy bun. Wow, she was a beautiful woman. Inside and out.

"Thanks for letting me sleep in," she murmured, leaning down to kiss Dominic's forehead before her lips met mine. Her gratitude warmed me, a balm to the chill of the spectral battles we faced.

"Now look. You've got me trapped. I've got our son in my arms. You know I can't chase you." My attempts at flirting were always lame.

"Haha. I got you right where I want you. How about some breakfast instead? Unless you had Cheerios too?"

"No to the cereal. Breakfast sounds great. We'll need all the energy we can get today," I replied, smiling despite the gravity of our situation. She nodded, her eyes reflecting the same resolve that fueled my own. She immediately started the coffee pot and began frying bacon and eggs.

"We're bringing Dominic to the office today," she decided, with a playful seriousness in her tone. "He might as well start his training young."

I chuckled, the sound mingling with Dominic's contented coos. "Might turn out to be the youngest ghost hunter in history," I replied with a chuckle.

We quickly ate our breakfast and eventually I handed Dominic over to her as I began to prepare for the day. We passed in the shower, dressed quickly and packed our son's bag.

The normalcy of these morning rituals, of feeding and dressing and readying ourselves, was grounding. Yet, beneath it all, the anticipation of the day's challenges lingered, a silent undercurrent to our domestic tranquility.

We piled into the SUV, the morning light casting long shadows across the road as we headed towards the Gulf Coast Paranormal office. The air was crisp, filled with the salty tang of Mobile Bay, a stark contrast to the darkness we were about to delve back into.

Cassidy sat beside me, Dominic was secured in his car seat. I could see his eyes taking in everything with wide curiosity.

Upon arriving, I watched as the team trickled in one by one, each person carrying the weight of last night's revelations a little differently. Joshua was the first to arrive, followed closely by Sierra, her eyes shadowed but determined. She'd stopped to pick up pastries. I ate one even though my wife raised an eyebrow at me.

We gathered around the large table in the conference room, the walls lined with monitors displaying the static-filled footage from the investigation. As the playback began, the room fell into a hushed silence. Each frame, each distorted audio clip seemed to thicken the air around us.

"We need to piece this together," I started, pointing to a segment where Francis appeared to speak directly to Helene. "Look at the interactions here—Francis's anguish, Helene's despair. It's all connected to the land the tower was built on."

Jericho interrupted, "It's that chapel that stirred it up. I don't know why, it's not like we don't have similar places like this in Mobile and Mobile County, but for some reason this place really caught this entity's attention."

The team nodded, their attention fixed as we analyzed the clips, noting every anomaly, every whispered word. "Helene... she's the one I feel sorry for the most," I confessed, watching a flicker of her image on the screen. Her face, full of sorrow and longing, haunted me more than the shadows.

Macie spoke sadly, "Think of all the Helenes in the past and in the present who are shunned for their faith. We think these things only happened during the witch trials in Salem and in Great Britain. Guess again. Mobile is notorious for its...religiosity...for lack of a better word."

With a clearer understanding of the spiritual dynamics at play, we shifted to strategizing our next move. "We need a precise and cautious approach," I instructed, pulling up a digital map of the haunted site on the screen. "Helene's spirit is key, and our intervention must be surgical."

At that moment, Chris walked in, slightly disheveled but with a spark in his eyes that had been missing the last time I saw him.

"Glad you could join us," I greeted him, clapping him on the shoulder. "We've got a tough one, but I think it's just what you need to get back into the swing of things." I could see Joshua's quizzical look but since when did I need anyone's permission to bring someone onto the team? As far as I knew, I was still the boss. Well, sometimes.

Chris nodded, a determined look crossing his face as he took in the room full of serious faces and eerie footage. "I'm ready, guys," he stated, his voice firmer than it had been in months.

"We're planning a rescue operation for tonight," I continued, outlining the plan. "I was lucky to get us one more day. I put Cal in a difficult position but we can do this. We'll use the evidence we've gathered to weaken the spirit's hold and create a window to communicate directly with Helene's spirit. Chris, your experience with emotional entities will be crucial."

As the team leaned in, scribbling notes and whispering amongst themselves, the weight of our task seemed to solidify. This wasn't just another investigation; it was a chance to right a wrong, to free a soul that had been bound in torment for centuries.

The room pulsed with a renewed energy, each member of the team motivated by the evidence and the plan that lay before us.

As the day wore on and our plans solidified, I announced that we'd finish our investigation into the property outside. "The residents will be returning soon, and we don't want to be in the way or cause any more distress than we've already done," I explained. Everyone nodded in agreement, understanding the delicacy and urgency of our situation.

Joshua and Chris began to set up the RYDER technology in the back of our equipment truck. The RYDER—a sophisticated spectral analysis tool—was something we hadn't used for a while but its ability to pinpoint and analyze spiritual energies would be crucial in the tower's complex environment. Or outside. I'd just about made up my mind to walk the land and stay out of the building.

"I'll wear the helmet," Joshua offered, stepping towards the device with a readiness that spoke of his usual willingness to dive into the unknown.

"No, let me do it," Chris interjected, a rare edge of eagerness in his voice. "I'm free now. Really. I promise. Let me try." It was a declaration of his readiness to face whatever came next, a testament to his journey back from his own shadows.

I watched as Chris fitted the helmet over his head, adjusting the sensors that would allow him to perceive and interact with the spiritual traces more directly. It was a gamble, but Chris's newfound resolve gave me hope that it was the right choice. Joshua glanced at me as I nodded my approval. He tapped on the screen, and we could all see what Chris could see.

The sun was beginning to set, casting a golden glow over the old cedar trees that dotted the property.

With the RYDER now fully operational, Chris began to walk slowly through certain spots around the building, including the orchard, the helmet's readouts flickered with activity.

We followed at a cautious distance, watching as the device's signals grew stronger, converging on a particularly dense part of the orchard.

The air grew tenser, the earlier excitement giving way to a heavy anticipation of what we might find.

"There!" Chris pointed towards a gnarled cedar, its branches hanging low, creating a natural canopy. As we approached, the outline of a figure became visible, huddled against the trunk, almost a part of the shadow itself.

It was Francis. His form was shrunken, diminished by shame and fear, his eyes wide and darting. We could all see him on the tablet. He was a pitiful figure. As we drew closer, it was clear he was not just hiding—he was bound, in a metaphysical sense, to the very spot, as if the roots of the tree itself held him captive.

His voice was a hoarse whisper when he saw us, a mix of relief and terror. "Help me," he pleaded, his gaze flickering between each of us and something unseen, hovering in the air around him.

The RYDER's screens buzzed with a chaotic pattern, signaling the intense spiritual energy that enveloped him. Chris knelt beside Francis, his hand extended in a gesture of support, his face set in a determined frown.

"We're here to help you, Francis. You're not alone in this anymore. You can be free."

As we prepared to break the spiritual chains binding him, I could feel the weight of the entity watching us, its presence a cold shadow against the fading light.

Oh no. This wasn't going to be easy at all.

This was it—the beginning of the confrontation we had prepared for, and our chance to free not just a tormented soul, but to reclaim a piece of ourselves lost in the shadows.

Chris's eyes locked onto the tormented man's face.

"Francis, I know what it's like," he began, his voice steady but filled with a raw honesty. "The shame, the feeling of being trapped by your past actions—it can consume you."

Chris paused, taking a deep breath as he shared a part of his own journey back from the edge. "I've been there, where you are, believing that forgiveness is impossible. But you have to start by forgiving yourself."

Francis's eyes, wide and fearful, flickered with a spark of recognition. Chris's words seemed to reach him, stirring something deep within. "It's the only way forward, Francis. It's the only way to break free from this entity," Chris urged.

However, the grip of the religious spirit was strong, and Francis's initial reaction shifted from one of hopefulness to one of hostility. He recoiled from Chris, his voice rising in a mix of despair and anger. The apparition began to flutter in and out of view on the tablet.

"No! You don't understand! You cannot!" he shouted, the spirit's influence pulsating around him like a dark aura. "You do not know what I have done. My wife—my child! I let them...they killed them! I killed them! If she would only listen! I could have saved her, but she refused. She made her choice! I couldn't help her!"

Chris persisted, undeterred by the fierce backlash. "I do understand, Francis. You were afraid."

" More than you know," he insisted, his tone softening.

Despite the hostility, Chris's presence was unyielding, a steady force against the storm of Francis's turmoil.

At this critical juncture, Sierra stepped forward, her expression focused and serene. Her slicked back blonde ponytail swung slightly as she moved. "We're going to need help, Midas. The guilt is too much."

I didn't argue the point. I felt she was right. Sierra closed her eyes, obviously reaching out with her psychic abilities to the ether. The air around us thickened, charged with a palpable energy as Sierra murmured softly, her words weaving through the twilight.

Chapter Seventeen—Sierra

"Helene, spirit bound by sorrow and injustice, hear my call," I whispered, my voice a melodic echo mingling with the air itself. "Come forth, show yourself, and aid us in this hour of need. Let your light guide the lost back to peace. Show mercy, Helene. Mercy that you never received, but have the power to give."

As my invocation stirred the air, a gentle wind began to rustle the leaves of the old cedar trees. Strangely, the scent of cedar awakened me, spiritually. The atmosphere brimmed with anticipation, all of us were holding our breath to see if she'd actually come.

To be honest, it would be difficult to forgive your husband for abandoning you, refusing to protect you and your child, but this situation had to end. If not for Helene, Francis, and the baby, at least for Cal, Sarah and the residents of the tower.

Then, emerging so subtly at first, a faint silhouette materialized beside Francis—the ethereal form of Helene. I kept my eyes closed but I could "see" her quite clearly.

Her appearance rippled through the charged air, a serene contrast to the dark energy swirling around Francis. Her expression carried a sorrowful yet calm wisdom, her eyes reflecting deep sadness, narrating untold stories and long-held pain.

My heart ached at the sight of the baby Helene cradled in her arms, wrapped in an old-fashioned lace and cotton blanket. Francis, still engulfed in his turmoil, appeared momentarily oblivious to her manifestation. How could he not see her?

Look, Francis! Helene is here.

As Helene's form grew more distinct and tangible, her gaze met Francis's—empathetic, sorrowful. The air vibrated with an unspoken dialogue, a silent exchange between the haunted and the haunter. He turned away from her, his agonizing scream said it all. I couldn't imagine being Francis in life or death.

"Francis," I called out, my voice now firm, trying to steer the reunion, "look beside you. Helene is here. She has heard our call and yours. Let her presence ease your spirit and release the binds of your captivity. You have to look at her. Look at your wife, Francis."

Nearby, in the shadow of the orchard, loomed another entity—tall, clad in black, and menacing. I didn't have to open my eyes to visualize him. I reached for Joshua's arm to steady myself.

"Joshua," I whispered cautiously. "It's here. The spirit—the Man in Black!" We should have known that an entity as powerful as a Religious Spirit would not go quietly into the night. Still, he had been partially defeated.

Even though his presence filled me with an uneasy fear, I watched as Helene stepped closer to Francis, her ethereal hand poised as if to caress his cheek, offering a solace and forgiveness that only those grievously wronged could grant.

Helene? Is that really you? Helene, I failed you.

To my surprise, she reached her pale hand toward him, her face serene and peaceful. This gesture seemed to pierce the veil of darkness around Francis, reaching deep into something long confined under layers of fear and manipulation.

Helene's spirit moved nearer to her husband, her outstretched hand touched Francis's gray cheek. As she touched him, I could see the evil that held Francis break. His posture softened, tears replaced the fierceness in his eyes as he and Helene reconnected.

"Je suis desolee," he murmured, his voice laden with the weight of his grief. "I am sorry. I am so sorry."

Helene nodded gently, her face etched with profound sadness yet tinged with compassion, as if to say, "I know, Francis. I know," though no words were spoken between them. Enveloped by Helene's presence, the dark aura around Francis began to fade, its grip lessening in the light of her forgiveness.

I finally opened my eyes and was overjoyed to see that I could continue to observe them. That wasn't always true as a psychic. I often work with impressions, thoughts, and glimmers of images.

Chris and the rest of the crew observed through the RYDER tablet—a blend of relief and awe visible in our expressions, as the shadows of Francis's shame started to dissolve.

The atmosphere lightened, as if a heavy burden had been lifted. And indeed it was being lifted right before our eyes. With the task complete, I relaxed my shoulders. Chris stood up, stepping aside to allow Francis and Helene a moment of reconciliation as he disengaged the RYDER.

This was the pivotal moment we had all worked toward—a cathartic release promising not only Francis's liberation but healing for all spirits ensnared in this haunted tale.

Yet, it wasn't over. As the poignant apex of Helene and Francis's reunion unfolded before my eyes, a moment of profound recognition transpired. Francis's weary gaze drifted downward to the delicate figure nestled in Helene's arms—their baby, swaddled in a fine lace blanket.

The sight ignited a transformative spark of joy and palpable relief across his face, a stark transformation from the haunted expression he had worn just moments before. I couldn't help but cry, completely ungracefully.

With a gentle touch, Helene extended her free hand towards Francis. He reached back, his hand trembling slightly, and clasped hers.

Together, as if guided by a celestial choreography, they began to move towards a radiant, shimmering light that materialized just for them. "Thank you, God," I whispered as I witnessed their transition. It was as though the universe itself had paused, creating a portal marked by hope and redemption.

As they walked forward, their physical forms gradually lost their sharpness, their edges blurring into the intense light that enveloped them. The light seemed to cleanse and lift them, carrying away the years of sorrow and turmoil that had weighed down their spirits.

The pair of them transformed into mere silhouettes against the overwhelming brilliance, their features softened and ethereal.

Helene, holding their child close, turned her head for one last look at me.

Her lovely eyes, brimming with peace and a silent gratitude, met mine. It was a farewell without words, a silent acknowledgment of the closure they had found. I found myself waving with my fingers gently.

Then, stepping fully into the light, they vanished, the brilliance snapping shut behind them like the soft closing of a book.

In that moment, standing there in the quiet aftermath, I felt a stirring mix of relief and awe. Helene and Francis, with their child, had crossed over to a realm of peace, their spirits liberated from the earthly bonds that had tormented them.

It was an ending and a beginning all at once, and the air around us seemed to whisper of both a resolved past and a hopeful future.

As the tranquil scene of departure unfolded with Helene, Francis, and their child stepping into the light, a sudden shift in the atmosphere occurred. And it happened much more quickly than I anticipated.

The Man in Black, fueled by a seething mix of fury and denial, erupted into a violent charge. His figure, cloaked in shadows, became a blur of dark energy that cut starkly through the serene glow surrounding the family.

Seeing him move at such speed made me sick.

The entity's movement was desperate and unrestrained, a dark specter racing against the inevitability of peace. The ground seemed to tremble under the force of his intent, each stride an echo of thwarted malice. He was hatred incarnate.

However, his efforts were in vain; as he reached the very spot where Helene and Francis had just stood, their figures had already begun to dissolve into the brilliant light.

Somehow, I knew that he would never have Francis again.

With the timing of a cruel joke, the light snapped shut the instant he arrived.

The portal closed with definitive clarity, leaving him lunging forward into nothing but empty air. There he stood, a figure of darkness momentarily suspended in a futile reach, his hands grasping at the void where the family had been seconds before. In the darkness, he screamed in anger.

His fury, once a terrifying force, now seemed palpable and impotent. The air around him crackled with the remnants of his thwarted energy, his body heaving with heavy, ragged breaths of frustration.

Strange that a dead thing would pretend to breathe.

The scene was a vivid contrast: the serene passage of spirits finding peace and the harsh desperation of darkness rebuffed at the threshold of light. It was a moment that underscored the victory of Light over Darkness, leaving the Man in Black to contend with his own echoing rage in the silent aftermath.

Reeling from his failed assault, the Man in Black spun towards us, his form still shrouded in the remnants of thwarted malice. His eyes blazed with a zealous fury, an unholy light that seemed to cast deeper shadows around him.

Fixing his burning gaze on Midas and Jericho, he unleashed his rage.

"You fools," he spat venomously, his voice booming and echoing off the bare trees around us with a chilling resonance. "You meddle with things beyond your reckoning! You are sinners, all of you, tampering with the divine order! God will judge you for this! Come to the true faith or perish! Bow the knee, you bastards!"

His words were laced with a fanatical righteousness, the fervor of a zealot consumed by his own distorted beliefs.

Jericho shouted back at him, "You do not represent God! You have no idea what the divine order looks like! Go back to the darkness from whence you came!"

The Man in Black stared at us with pure hatred. His stance was menacing, a dark figure looming larger as he stepped forward, the ground beneath him seemingly recoiling from his touch. He swore as he moved toward us.

"Everyone get back," Midas shouted and we all obeyed. Except Jericho, he was digging in his bag and pulled out a pendant and slim bible. Seeing the objects apparently pissed the Man in Black off. He immediately began to swear angrily.

Each word that erupted from the Man in Black was laden with the weight of condemnation and threat, dripping with venom and echoing ominously through the chilling air.

His inhuman voice, a harsh and grating sound, seemed to warp the space around us, the words cutting through the silence like shards of glass. I wanted to cover my ears so I didn't have to hear him again.

His presence was oppressively heavy, a tangible darkness that seemed to thicken the very atmosphere. It felt as though the air itself was recoiling, trying to escape his reach, yet being pulled inexorably back towards him.

As he threw random, yet condemning biblical verses at us, the space around us became charged, the ambient energies of the night warping in response to his malevolence.

Shadows seemed to gather more densely around him, as if drawn by his dark energy, making him appear larger and more formidable. The trees around us swayed slightly, their movements not caused by any breeze but seemingly in reaction to the force of his anger, their branches trembling as if in fear or anticipation.

As he continued to spew his threats, the oppressive nature of his being seemed to seep into our very bones, the coldness of his words chilling us from the inside out. It was as if his presence was not just an external threat but something that could invade, corrupt, and chill to the core.

Each breath we took felt heavier, laden with the dread of his next utterance, the air thick with the dark promise of his continued wrath.

The air crackled with the intensity of his conviction, as if his mere words could invoke divine wrath upon us. His threats, ringing with the certainty of a man blinded by his own faith, reverberated through the chilling night, casting a pall over the temporary peace we had just witnessed. His demeanor was not just of anger but of a deep, unyielding hatred, the kind that festers and spreads, threatening to engulf everything in its path.

Jericho seemed rattled but he didn't pause long. I clutched Joshua's hand, just as Cassidy was standing side by side with Midas. Jericho raised his slim bible and his pendant and began to shout.

"By the Light that governs day and night, by the sacred Light that protects us from spite, we command you, leave this place—now banished from our presence. From God's presence!" His voice, firm and unyielding, echoed through the clearing, a beacon of resolve.

Beside him, Macie joined in, her voice harmonizing with Jericho's, lending strength and depth to the invocation. "Shadows retreat, darkness dissolves; by these words, we decree your resolve. We sever you from earth and sky, in the name of the Light, we bid you goodbye!"

The combined force of their words seemed to create a palpable energy barrier, a shimmering wall of sound and intent that encircled the Man in Black. He laughed again, a sound meant to unsettle, but his laughter faltered as the force of the prayer began to take hold.

The atmosphere thickened, charged with the power of our unified command.

As Jericho and Macie continued, repeating the phrase again and again, we began to do the same. It was an easy invocation to remember.

Finally, the air around the Man in Black shimmered with a faint luminescence, the very particles of the night air vibrating with the energy of the sacred words. ""By the Light that governs day and night, by the sacred Light that protects us from spite, we command you, leave this place—now banished from our presence. From God's presence!"

"No! You cannot command me!"

The Man in Black's form flickered under the weight of the chant, his figure distorting as if caught between realms. The shadows that had seemed so solid began to dissipate, pulled apart by the magnetic pull of the banishment spell. His defiance turned to frustration, his sneers to grunts of effort as he fought against the spiritual lasso that sought to drag him from our presence.

"No!"

With each repeat of their words, our confidence grew, and the light within the circle brightened, a visible sign of the prayer's potency. His presence, once a formidable shadow casting dread, now waned, reduced to a mere whisper of malice fading into the ether.

"Be gone, foul spirit, by light compelled, this ground you'll haunt no more," Jericho concluded, his voice a final, decisive strike. As he spoke, he threw the bible at the entity, and it landed in front of him with a thud.

Silence fell over us, heavy and profound, as we processed the immediate relief of his absence. The prayer had worked—his malevolence expelled, at least for now, restoring a fragile peace to the haunted night.

The Man in Black responded to our efforts with a disdainful laugh, a sound so cold it seemed to freeze the very air, echoing around us like the chime of a death knell. But I could hear the defeat in his voice. This was not going to go well for him.

"You do not have the authority to banish me," he sneered, his voice a harsh rasp that scraped against our nerves. His form, though momentarily flickering like a faulty shadow cast by flickering firelight, quickly steadied, a testament to his seemingly unshakable presence. "I have been here long before you came and I will be here long after your bones decay."

Yet, as we intensified our chant, the air around him began to quiver, as if the fabric of reality itself was being strained. His silhouette started to waver more noticeably, edges blurring and sharpening in a rapid, unsettling rhythm.

It was as if our words, our unified spirit of defiance, were physically affecting the space he occupied. His dark eyes darted between Jericho and Macie, a flicker of uncertainty crossing his otherwise impassive face. The shadows that clung to him seemed to swirl in turmoil, as if confused and agitated by the conflicting energies of our sacred chants and his dark aura.

"By the Light that governs day and night, by the sacred Light that protects us from spite, we command you, leave this place—now banished from our presence. From God's presence!" Cassidy, Macie and I shouted the prayer as the men continued to stand their ground.

As our voices rose, the surrounding night intensified in darkness, concentrating the battle of light and shadow into our very circle.

The Man in Black, now visibly struggling to maintain his composure, threw his head back and let out a defiant roar, a last attempt to assert his dominance. However, our words only grew louder, the chant becoming a powerful crescendo that filled the clearing, the trees themselves seeming to lean inwards, drawn by the force of our plea for purity and release.

With one final push, his figure flickered rapidly, like a storm-damaged lantern struggling to stay lit in a tempest.

"This is not the end of me!" he shouted, his voice breaking through his rapidly weakening form. But his threat was cut short as his image finally shattered, like a glass pane cracked by a relentless hail, his presence dissolving into the night, leaving behind a tense but victorious silence.

We stood there, breathless, and wary, knowing that while we had won this battle, the war against such darkness was far from over.

But for now, we had achieved a moment of respite, a brief pause in our ongoing struggle against the unseen forces that lurked just beyond the veil of our reality.

We had just gone to battle with the Spirit of Religion and although he'd been pushed back and away from the tower, was still alive in Mobile. If you could call it that. Religion had been here a long time.

At least for now, he would no longer be able to torment these poor people and better yet, Helene and Francis now had peace.

That was worth everything.

Author's Note

Dear Readers,

Thank you for joining me once again in the eerie and mysterious world of Gulf Coast Paranormal. It is has been my joy to bring you on dozens of paranormal investigations with our favorite investigators.

"Tower of Darkness," Book One of Season Three, promises to continue the chilling adventures you've come to love, set against the haunting backdrop of the Gulf Coast. This season will be inspired by the rich ghostly history of the region and explores deeper, darker secrets that lurk in the shadows. And there are so many secrets in those shadowy places, aren't there?

The theme of the "Spirit of Religion" plays a significant role in this installment. It's a concept I've pondered deeply over the years—how the intense adherence to religious doctrines can sometimes lead to a type of zealotry that overshadows the essence of true spirituality. I've experienced this cruel spirit myself multiple times in my lifetime. Using people's faith to control them, to cause and cruelty is the height of evil.

I aimed to dissect the thin line that can exist between faith and fanaticism. It is a horrible place to be. In my opinion, faith reveals and embraces unconditional love. Religious fanaticism offers a form of love with conditions. It's a sick and twisted spirit but unfortunately so pervasive in many areas of the world.

The Spirit of Religion is real and dangerous, as you'll discover through the twists and turns of this story. It's a cautionary tale that reminds us that being spiritual and having faith in God does not require us to become zealots.

True spirituality is about compassion, understanding, and connection to Someone greater than ourselves, without losing our humanity in the process. God is the very essence of love.

I hope "Tower of Darkness" resonates with you as much as it has with me. I am eager to hear your thoughts and interpretations, and I am grateful for your continued support.

Thank you for being part of this journey. There are more secrets to uncover, and I can't wait to explore them with you in the upcoming books.

Warmest regards,

M.L. Bullock

If you want to connect with me at a deeper level, please feel free to email me at authormlbullock@gmail.com or become a follower of my Facebook fan page at www.facebook.com/authormlbullock.com[1].

---

1. http://www.facebook.com/authormlbullock.com

Don't miss out!

Visit the website below and you can sign up to receive emails whenever M.L. Bullock publishes a new book. There's no charge and no obligation.

https://books2read.com/r/B-A-CXMC-RNUMD

BOOKS 2 READ

Connecting independent readers to independent writers.

Also by M.L. Bullock

Create and Prosper
The Prolific Writer: How to Write and Create a Successful Catalog of Books

Desert Queen Saga
The Tale of Nefret
The Falcon Rises
The Kingdom of Nefertiti
The Song of the Bee Eater

Devecheaux Antiques and Haunted Things Trilogy Series
A Cup of Shadows
A Voice From Her Past
A Watch Of Weeping Angels

Gulf Coast Paranormal
The Ghosts of Kali Oka Road
The Ghosts of the Crescent Theater

A Haunting on Bloodgood Row
The Legend of the Ghost Queen
A Haunting at Dixie House
The Ghost Lights of Forrest Field
The Ghost of Gabrielle Bonet
The Ghost of Harrington Farm
The Creature on Crenshaw Road
A Ghostly Ride in Gulfport
The Ghosts of Phoenix No.7
The Maelstrom of the Leaf Academy
The Ghosts of Oakleigh House
The Spirits of Brady Hall
The Gray Lady of Wilmer

Gulf Coast Paranormal Season Two
The Wayland Manor Haunting
The Beast of Limerick House
The Beast of Limerick House
A Haunting at Goliath Cave
Death Among the Roses
The Captain of Water Street
Return to the Leaf Academy

Gulf Coast Paranormal Trilogy Series
Ghosted
Haunted
Dead
Spooked
Paranormal

Haunting Passions
For the Love of Shadows
Her Haunted Heart

Idlewood
The Ghosts of Idlewood
Dreams of Idlewood
The Whispering Saint
The Haunted Child

Laurel House
Whispers

Lost Camelot
Guinevere Unconquered
The Undead Queen of Camelot

Lost Camelot Trilogy
Guinevere Forever

Marietta
The Bones of Marietta
Footsteps of Angels

Morgans Rock
The Haunting of Joanna Storm
The Hall of Shadows
The Ghost of Joanna Storm

Return to Seven Sisters
The Roses of Mobile
All the Summer Roses
Blooms Torn Asunder
A Garden of Thorns
Wreath of Roses

Scary Fall Stories
Horrible Little Things

Seven Sisters
Seven Sisters
Moonlight Falls On Seven Sisters
Shadows Stir At Seven Sisters
The Stars That Fell
The Stars We Walked Upon
The Sun Rises Over Seven Sisters
Beyond Seven Sister
Ghost on a Swing

Shabby Hearts
A Touch Of Shabby
Shabbier By The Minute
Shabby By Night
Shabby All The Way
Star Spangled Shabby

Southern Gothic
Being With Beau
Death's Last Darling
Spook House

Southland
Southland

Sugar Hill
Wife Of The Left Hand
Fire On The Ramparts
Blood By Candlelight
The Starlight Ball
His Lovely Garden

Summerleigh
The Belles of Desire, Mississippi

The Ghost Of Jeoprady Belle
The Lady In White
Loxley Belle

Supernatural Support Group
Circle of Shadows

The Mummy Queen's Revenge
Queen Mummy

Twelve to Midnight
Mary Twelves

Standalone
The Hauntings of Idlewood
Lost Camelot
The Desert Queen Collection
Haunting Passions
Ghosts on a Plane
Halloween Screams
Dead Is the Loneliest Place to Be
River Run
Tower of Darkness
Believer's Guide to Paranormal Ministry

About the Author

Author M.L. Bullock enjoys the laid-back atmosphere and the spooky vibe of the Gulf Coast, especially the region's historic districts and sites. When she isn't visiting her favorite haunts in New Orleans or Old Mobile, you can find her flipping through old photographs or newspaper clippings in search of new inspiration.

Read more at www.mlbullock.com.

www.ingramcontent.com/pod-product-compliance
Lightning Source LLC
Chambersburg PA
CBHW050517160726
48003CB00001B/338